Where is Emma?

by Taylor Storm

Taylor Storm

taylorstormtaylor@gmail.com

TABLE OF CONTENTS

Chapter 1

"I love you," said a girl with long brown hair. She lay in bed with one arm under her head.

"I love you too, Emma," said Michael Danes. He brushed her hair with his hand. They cuddled together under the sheets as the morning light seeped in from the windows.

"Michael?" a voice called from behind the bedroom door. "Is that you? Are you home?"

"I'll be right there," Michael said over his shoulder.

"Michael?" a knock on the door made Michael groan.

"I'm coming, I'm coming." He turned around and found his bed empty. "Emma?"

"Michael!"

Michael stirred in bed. He opened his eyes, then rubbed a hand over his face.

"Michael!"

"I'm awake, Mom!" Michael yelled. He threw off the covers and got out of bed; he stood half naked in front of his window.

Nick, the neighbor's ten-year old kid stared at Michael from across the street.

Michael gave him the finger. Nick stuck his tongue out and biked away. Michael drew in the curtains and pulled on his jeans, buttoned up his shirt and opened the door.

"It's ten in the morning!" Michael's mother scolded from the kitchen.

"Mom, I'm twenty-one years old!" Michael said. "I can wake up any damn time I want." He walked into the bathroom and brushed his teeth.

"Your college has been calling all day!" Michael's mom yelled from the kitchen.

Michael rolled his eyes. He saw his reflection in the mirror and spat into the sink. Michael grabbed his bag from the hallway and headed into the kitchen. He snatched a donut off the counter.

"Hey! Sit down and eat your breakfast. I didn't cook for nothing." Michael's mom, a woman of fifty-something, tipped the pan over and scraped scrambled eggs onto a plate.

Michael picked up the plate and walked out the kitchen door; he turned around and grabbed the door before it slammed shut just in time to say, "thanks, mom!"

Michael headed around the house and over to the driveway. His black Toyota Corolla, almost ten years old, was rusting away on the driveway. He put his plate on the hood of the car, opened the door, and got in. He looked to the passenger seat and saw a stack of flyers with a girl's picture on them. The title read, "Have You Seen Me?" followed with "Emma Styles, missing since November 5th."

Michael grabbed the papers and shoved them onto the dashboard of his car, then put his keys in the ignition.

"Come on, come on," Michael urged. The engine finally came alive. He put the car in reverse and froze. "Shit!" He rolled down the window, grabbed his plate off the roof of his car and proceeded to pull out of the driveway.

Within ten minutes, he pulled into the parking lot. Students walked across campus, chatting, reading. When Michael stepped out of the car, some stared at him. He grabbed the posters off his dashboard, his plate sat empty in the passenger seat. He'd gotten used to having food on the go.

Michael distributed posters to people he came across on his way to the building. "Please call this number when you find her. Thanks!"

As soon as he reached the front door, Michael was stopped by a man with glasses.

"Mr. Danes," he said. "I need you to come with me, immediately."

Michael rolled his eyes. He followed the man inside and into the on-campus security office.

"Hanging posters on the premises is impermissible," said the man to the security officer at the desk. "I've told him a hundred times; can you make it any clearer to him? Do something for God's sake. I'm paying you to do your job."

The officer bit her lip. "Mr. Danes," she said, folding her hands over her desk.

"Michael's fine."

"Mr. Danes," continued the officer. "You see this?" She pointed to a flashing red light on her office phone. "That's twelve voice messages. You know from who?"

"Your boyfriend," Michael snickered.

A hand slammed against the table. "This is no laughing matter Mr. Danes," yelled the man with glasses.

"Chris," said the officer, looking at the man with glasses, "don't you have a class to attend to?"

"You don't need to talk me into getting out of here. I was just leaving anyway," Chris growled. "If I see you one more time—"

"Of course, you're going to see me often," Michael interrupted. "I go to school here. Well, until I graduate this June."

"I'm going to make sure you'll never leave this college until you stop this nonsense behavior. Your girlfriend dumped you. Just accept it and admit it."

"Emma did not break up with me." Michael stood up.

"Keep telling yourself that." Chris slammed the door behind him as he walked away.

"Mr. Danes, have a seat," the officer said. "Emma's parents have been calling all day. Their daughter is not missing."

"So, they say," Michael rolled his eyes.

"She called them on November fifth and told them she would be going to visit her aunt in Florida."

"See, that's exactly why she's missing. Emma would never do that."

"Do what, Mr. Danes? Leave you? Without a phone call? Without talking to you first? Kind of makes me wonder what you did to a girl to treat you like that."

"I was with Emma the night before she left. She looked scared. She wouldn't tell me what was wrong."

"Perhaps she wanted to break up with you then," the officer said. "I see it happen all the time. This is Oakland, Indiana, Mr. Danes. Not much else goes on here."

"I'm telling you, Emma has been missing for three days now. It's only a thirteen-hour drive to Florida. She would have been at her aunt's by now. Her aunt would have called, don't you think?"

"You have a point, Mr. Danes," the officer said. "I'll tell you what if the next call doesn't come in from her end, I'll make a personal call to that aunt of hers and find out if she's there or not. All right?"

"Thank you," Michael said. He got up and left. He headed to the notice boards in the field. "Chris, you jerk," he said upon seeing the posters of Emma taken down. He nailed a few more and distributed the rest to oncoming students.

"Hey!" a voice yelled from across the field.

"Shit." Michael made a run for it.

"Come back here!" Chris yelled.

Michael got into the car and drove off. He went to a nearby gas station, filled up his car and headed inside.

"Jake," Michael called from the door.

"Hey, dude," a man replied from behind the cashier. "How's it going? Still looking for your girl?"

"Yeah," Michael said. He taped a poster to the window of the gas station.

"She didn't call you yet?"

"No. It keeps going to voicemail. You think we can gather up the gang tonight and start like a…search team?"

Jake spat. "You serious?"

"Jake, I'm damn serious, man. She's missing. Emma is not the kind of girl to just run off without telling anyone."

"Her parents said she called them."

"Lies, all lies. They know she's not at her aunt's, and everyone's going to know when the next call doesn't come through. It's been three days. There's no way she's going to Florida." Michael grabbed a granola bar off the shelf under the counter. He unwrapped it.

"You want me to pay for that?"

"That okay? I spent thirty cents per poster."

"Why don't you just take an ad out in the paper?"

"Costs a lot of money."

"Just get Jess on it," said Jake. "She's got connections with *Oakland News*. She can get them to do it."

"Sweet," Michael said. He picked up his phone and called Jessica while chewing on the bar. It went to voice mail. "Hi,

Jess, it's Michael. I'm at Jake's now, the station. You free to talk? Come on over to Jake's." Michael checked with Jake, then nodded, "tonight. It's about Emma."

"Did you speak with Emma's friends?"

Michael hung up. "No, man. She doesn't have any friends. Even if she did, no one knows her like I do."

"Two years and you'd think she'd explain herself," said Jake. "That's tough."

"We all knew her much longer than that." Michael remembered when Emma first moved into Oakland back when he was in middle school. She had a long brown braid down the side of her neck and wore a collared dress. Mrs. Fran had welcomed her as the "girl who moved from New York."

Emma was a city girl when Michael first met her. She talked fast and used words like "presumptuous" and "impudent" to describe his friends and him whenever they asked her to come out and play. She never sat with them in the back of the classroom, but always in the front.

"So, I won't be able to see who's looking at me," she said. "I have my back to the class and I can avoid eye contact."

Once there was a rumor that Emma moved to Oakland because her parents were cheating on each other in New York. They moved down to Oakland to fix their relationship.

Emma hated the word "fix," but, she never quite explained her parents' story.

Michael was playing basketball with his friends during practice after school. When the ball rolled off to the lockers, he heard a cry.

"Who's there?" he said, picking up the ball. He tracked down the sound to a gym closet and opened it. "Emma?"

"Go away," she said, burying her face in her knees. "If you tell anyone, I will kill you."

"It's okay," he comforted. "You're my friend. Even if you don't think the same of me, you can still talk to me. What happened?"

"Scott happened."

"The school bully? What did he say now? The whole lie about your parents?"

"Not just that; everything."

"Don't worry. Everyone knows Scott is the world's biggest liar. No one ever believes a word he says."

"You're just being nice."

"It's true. Last year, I got hit by a door in the face. Scott told everyone I got punched by a girl."

Emma laughed. "No way."

"Yeah, you know what I did?"

"What?"

"I punched him in the face and his front tooth fell out. That'sh why he talksh like thish now."

Emma laughed.

"Who wantsh to lishten to someone who talksh like thish?"

Emma's tears dried up as she hugged her stomach and laughed. Michael found her beautiful.

"Now, come on." He stretched out his hand. "Let's get you out of this closet and back into the world."

Emma paused for a moment. "You know what…you're not as presumptuous as I thought you were." She took his hand.

"Thanks," he said, wondering if presumptuous was a good thing. He helped her up on her feet.

"Hey, Michael," a voice called from the door.

Emma and Michael let go of each other's hand.

"Did you get the ball?" a boy asked; he was wearing a basketball shirt. "Come on man, we're waiting on you."

"Yeah, I'm coming." He looked back at Emma. "Come hang out with us sometime, after school, or whenever."

"S-sure," she smiled.

"Michael! Come on, man!" the voice called again from the gym.

"Coming!" Michael yelled back. "See you later!"

"Michael," Jake said from the counter. "Your phone."

Michael snapped out of it. He was still in the station. His phone buzzed in his pocket.

Hello? Jess? Oh, awesome." Michael gave Jake the thumbs up. "Today? Yeah, I'll text you a picture right now. Sweet. See you tonight." He hung up and slammed the phone down on the counter. "Man! You're not going to believe it!"

"I think I will," said Jake.

Michael grabbed Jake's wrist.

"Woah, easy dude, that's not what I meant."

"It's almost one. Give me your phone."

"What?"

"You have a smartphone, right?"

"Yeah."

Michael, stretching his hands over the counter, pulled on Jake's jean pocket.

"Okay, okay, chill dude." Jake tossed him his phone. "Make it quick, okay? I don't want to be stuck in this dead zone, staring out the window."

Michael went to the touch screen and entered the password. Jake's birthday. He clicked on the internet browser as it started to load. He lifted the phone up to get more bars, in hopes of speeding up the internet.

"It's so boring out here. I need it to kill time, man," Jake continued.

Michael, with his hand up in the air, walked out the door.

"Hey, Michael, you listening to me? Oh, my God." Jake slapped his forehead.

Michael headed to the car. The local town page loaded, and he typed in "the girl who came in first place in Oakland's marathon."

An article popped up.

"Yes!" Michael yelled in the car. He drove off as he clicked on a picture. It was a younger version of Emma with shoulder-length hair. She had a band around her head, with sweat trickling down her face. He downloaded the picture.

"Three-thousand dollars, everyone," a man spoke into the microphone. "Emma Styles has raised three-thousand dollars by making this forty-kilometer run."

Emma hugged Michael at the finish line.

"You did it!" he said into her ear. "You really did it."

Emma panted over his shoulder. "Uh-huh."

"Here," Michael offered her a water bottle.

"Thanks." She poured it over her head and down her back.

"Can we have Emma Styles on the stage?" an announcer said into the microphone.

"We're so proud of you, honey," Emma's parents cheered from behind the sidelines. They then took her picture.

Emma headed onto the stage and shook hands with the principal of Oakland College. A few other founders of a charity shook hands with Emma. Emma held a big check of three-thousand dollars while the founders of a charity held the other end. They posed for the picture. The principal gave Emma a medal and tapped her on the shoulder.

"Can we have those who came in second and third place up here on stage?" the announcer continued as the runners lined up.

More people were crossing the finish line, while others were still far behind, walking.

The honk of a car startled Michael on the road. He pressed on the gas and headed past a green light. He looked at the phone. The picture had finished downloading. He sent it to Jessica.

"Got it," she texted him back. "It will be out in the Friday paper."

"What?" Michael said out loud. "No," he texted back. "It needs to be out now."

A police siren went off behind Michael.

"Damn it!" Michael tossed the phone onto the passenger's seat and pulled over. He checked his face in the rear-view mirror. rolled down his window and waited.

The police car door opened. An officer stepped out. "Is that you Danes?"

"Yes, sir!" he yelled back.

The officer walked over to the car. He had white scruffy, greying hair under his cap.

"I knew it was you. I just couldn't see you there because you had your head down. Figured you might be on your phone. You know son, you can't be using that while you're driving."

"I'm sorry, Steve," Michael said. "My girl is missing. I was just trying to get the word out to help find her."

"The Styles' girl?" Steve asked with his hands on his hips. "Okay, I'll tell you what. I'll put a word out on her at the precinct. See if anyone has seen her or knows something about her disappearance. I'd be careful of the Styles family if I were you, though. They're getting pretty angry with you."

"Thanks, Steve. I owe you one."

"You always do, kid. Now, stop using that phone and stay in school." Steve tapped Michael on the shoulder.

Michael saluted and drove on.

***

At Jake's, later that night, Michael took a beer out of the fridge.

Jake poured some chips into a bowl. Their friend Rob shuffled a deck of cards.

"Chris could not shut up about you all day," Rob said. "He pulled me out of class, wondering where you went."

"Yeah, I was hanging posters."

"Still? Dude? The Styles are pissed."

"If they cared at all about Emma they would be helping with the search," Michael said, taking a seat. "Perhaps they'd take me more seriously once they see the ad in the paper. Emma is out there, she might see it too."

"How'd you get the ad done?" Rob asked.

"Jess," Michael and Jake answered.

"No way." Rob's eyes widened. "What did she ask for it?"

Jake looked at Michael.

"Nothing."

"Wait, did you text her from my phone?" Jake asked. "Oh my God, Michael. And now she's coming here, to my house."

The front door opened. "Hello?!"

"Oh my God, that's her," Jake turned in his chair. "I can't believe you, Michael. You have to tell her."

A tall woman with a big build walked into the kitchen.

"Hi Jess, Jake texted you about the ad," Michael said.

"What?" Jake looked back at Michael. "No, Jess, it wasn't me. He took my phone."

Jess smiled. "It's fine."

"I'm so dead," Jake whispered to Michael.

"I did my best. It's on the website now, but it's going to be out tomorrow," Jess told the group. "I sent you the link. You can check it out." She took a seat at the table. "You got dip?" She grabbed a chip.

"Yeah, it's in the fridge." Jake pointed behind his back. "Okay, fine. I'll get it."

Michael looked at Jake's phone. "Great! So, let's go over what we remember on November fifth," Michael said, opening his notebook.

"I saw Emma in math class with Chris that morning," Rob said. "She had her usual coffee in hand—"

"Which she bought from the station where I was working," Jake added.

"Did she buy anything else?" Michael asked.

"Nope, she had exact change too; the usual."

"Okay, so she left her house in the morning, went to the station around eight-ish—"

"Eight twelve," Jake said. "I got the receipt, remember?"

"Right," Michael continued. "Which you still didn't give me, by the way. I need that as evidence."

"I can't just take receipts without my boss knowing," Jake complained.

"Make a copy, take a picture of it, put it in the system—"

"Okay, okay, man," Jake replied, putting the dip on the table. "It's all on camera anyways."

Michael's jaw dropped open.

"No way," Rob said. "There's a camera at the station and you're only telling us this now?"

Jake gasped. "Oh my God, I'm so sorry, guys. I totally forgot."

"Get the footage," Michael said. "Call your boss now and tell him we're coming over."

The doorbell rang.

"Are you expecting anyone?" Jess asked, munching on a chip.

"Dude, do I look like someone who gets a lot of visits?" Jake pointed to himself. He had an unshaven beard, long hair, and wore pajamas all the time when he wasn't at work. "My parents are always up in their bungalow and leave the house to me. Not even their friends and neighbors stop by."

The doorbell rang again.

"I'm coming!" Jake yelled. He pulled the door open. An older couple stormed in. Jake's eyes widened.

"Michael!" the older man called. "Where are you?" He marched into the kitchen. Michael, Rob, and Jess stared back from the table.

"Mr. Styles?" Michael pushed his chair back. "I-I can explain."

"You better," Mr. Styles said. He grabbed Michael by the collar. "You have gotten us into a lot of trouble, kid. I thought the school explained everything to you, but I still see pictures of my girl everywhere and now she's on some site, the *Oakland News*?!"

"I did that," Jess said. "I work for the paper."

Mr. Styles looked at Jess.

"Tom, stop it, you're hurting him," Mrs. Styles said, holding back her husband's arm.

"I told you a billion times to back off, but clearly you don't understand words!" Mr. Styles yelled, pushing Michael against the wall.

"Enough!" A fist banged against the table loudly. The table wobbled. The bowl of dip tipped over and to the edge. Jake caught it amidst the silence.

"This is an expensive carpet," he muttered.

Jess held her fist in the air. "I'll punch you both if you don't leave now."

"You falsely publicize things about my daughter, and now you threaten us?" Mrs. Styles yelled.

Jess walked up to Mr. Styles and eyed him up and down.

"Come on." Mr. Styles let go of Michael. "Let's get out of here. These kids aren't worth our time."

"What?" Mrs. Styles argued. "Are you kidding me? No, we're not leaving until this is done."

Mr. Styles grabbed his wife and pulled her behind him.

"This is not over!" she yelled at the group. "You have no right to threaten us. She's our daughter. You have no right to do this to us or to her! You hear me?!"

Rob closed the door after them. "Good riddance."

Michael slumped against the wall and onto the floor.

"Michael, you okay?" Jake asked.

Michael sighed. "I don't know guys, am I the only one who's crazy here? I was the last person Emma saw before she disappeared, right? Why do I have a bad feeling about this?"

"It's okay, dude. You're just worried about her—"

"No, man," Rob interrupted Jake. "She should have called. If she cared for any of us, for Michael, I mean we're her friends too, right? How could she just take off like that? And make everyone worry about her?"

"Exactly, Emma wouldn't do that," Jake argued.

"You know what I think?" Rob said, nervously taking out a cigarette.

"Don't do that in the house, man." Jake reached for the cigarette. Rob dodged.

"I think the Styles know."

"Know what?"

"Think about it." Rob put the cigarette in his mouth and lit it. "Why would they come in here and tell us to back off? Why are they so intent on keeping everything quiet? Come on, they know where Emma is. They're hiding something."

Chapter 2

Jess biked to work the next morning. She took her bike on the bus and headed downtown. She got off at the last stop and biked the rest of the way to *Oakland News*.

"Hi, boys," she said walking into the office. "Miss me?" She high-fived a colleague on her way to her desk.

"Did you see last night's game?" another colleague asked. "That touchback at the end, woo -hoo!" He applauded. "Gonna be on the first page of sports."

"Yeah, I missed it."

"What?" her colleague gaped. "Since when you miss a game?"

"Since yesterday," Jess replied. "Where's Stan?"

"In the back."

Jess headed into the storage room. "Stan? You there?"

"Back here," a voice replied. A box crashed onto the ground and tapes fell out.

"You okay? What are you doing?"

"Just looking through some old games," Stan mumbled. "Stupid boss wants me to refresh his memory about some game we got ourselves talking about. Thinks I'm wrong about the score."

"Who cares? Just tell him he's right and you're wrong. That's all he wants to hear anyway. How'd you think I get my bonuses?"

Stan smiled. "Right." He tapped her on the back. "I heard you went upstairs," Stan pointed up. "How was that?"

"Fine. Got the news on the website. Haven't seen the paper yet."

"I saw it," Stan added. "You really think she's missing? It's not just some runaway story?"

Jess shrugged.

"We still on for tonight?"

"Tonight?"

"Yeah at the bar, watching the game."

"Sure…oh, no wait. I got to go to the town's community gathering."

"You still go to that?"

"Yeah, it's just a bunch of women talking about their fears, I know. I just like to be there to motivate them to go out there and fight their battles, you know."

"And you don't have any fears to share?"

Jess smiled. "Right." She slapped him on the back. "Let's do it some other night."

"You sure?"

Jess headed out the door and gave him the thumbs up.

***

Later that evening, Jess biked to the community center.

"Hey ladies," she said through the door. "How's it kicking?"

"Jess!" A few ladies smiled back. They sat around tables playing poker. Some smoked, some drank, and others just played the game.

"How are you, Becky?" Jess asked her friend. "I haven't heard from you." She sat next to her.

Becky averted her eyes.

"Was it Ralph again?" Jess grabbed Becky's arm. "Did he hurt you?"

"I'm fine." Becky shook off Jess' arm. "It's not Ralph, it's Daniel. I don't want him growing up like his dad. I mean, the divorce has been finalized, but still. The man's just bad news and it's rubbing off on our child."

"He'll be fine," Jess assured. "I saw him play soccer last week."

"I got wrapped up in a case," Becky whispered. She covered her face. "I'm such a bad mom, I should be with him, spend more time with him."

"He's fifteen," Jess assured. "You had him when you were his age. You should see him with his friends…I mean, he actually has friends."

They both laughed.

"He's nothing like his dad. You'll see."

"I'm happy to hear that," Becky said, rolling the dice. "Wanna play?"

"Sure." Jess drew her cards. "So, last night, this old man tried to beat up a friend of a friend. I just held my fist up like this and told them to get out before I punched him and his wife."

"Ohhh," a few ladies commented. "Tell us more."

"Talk about men being so afraid of a woman getting the best of them."

A few laughed.

"You know one time," Anna, a woman in her forties with blackened teeth and white-blonde hair, spoke with a cigarette in her mouth. "I was at the bar, and this large dude, and I mean large, came over to me and asked for a dance. When he wouldn't buzz off, I put out my cigarette on his arm and told him his balls would be next."

The women laughed.

"Yeah, it's just like that one time," another woman, Stacy, said. "You know Jess, how you taught me to elbow a guy in the face? Yeah, well I did that a few days ago."

"To who?" Jess laughed.

"My ex-husband!" Stacy slapped the table.

"Again?"

"Well, I hate his face, every time he shows up, I just can't help it. It's like a reflex."

"Wow, I never had to resort to violence with my family," another added.

"With your husband?" Stacy asked.

"With my father-in-law," the woman continued. "Since I'm Indian, we have to live with our husband's family. My father-in-law is always trying to embarrass me in front of everyone. When he went to take his shower, I turned off the hot water. He kept knocking on the wall and asking for hot water. I just turned up the volume on my radio. When he came out with his bathrobe, freezing to death, and asked me if I had anything to do with it, I said, you mean it was as cold as you were to me yesterday?"

No one laughed.

"Damn, that's some hard shit right there," Becky said. The women laughed.

"Talk about women intimidating men, right?" Anna said. "I got a couple of those."

Anna went on to share with the rest of them.

Jess got a text from Jake. "You coming? We're all at the gas station."

"I'm gonna have to call it a night," Jess announced to the women.

"Oh, come on, we just started a new game." Stacy rolled her eyes.

"Is it a hot date of yours?" Anna purred.

"Ha, no, just a friend."

Anna put her hands in the air. "That's what they all say…until it's past midnight and the roof is on fire."

"Say hi to him for me," Stacy licked her lip.

Jess waved goodbye and went on her way. She biked ahead of traffic and caught the last bus. When she got off, she biked past a park. She stopped to examine the scratched rail.

A boy on his bike had crashed into it a long time ago, she remembered. More like pushed into it by Scott and his friends.

"Give us the money," yelled Scott from his bike.

"I don't have any!" The boy amidst the crash, knee-deep into the mud, said.

One of Scott's friends brought the wheel of his bike close to the boy's leg. "I'll break it," he warned.

"Do it," Scott said. "I'd love to see him cry."

The boy closed his eyes.

"Oww," Scott screamed.

The boy opened his eyes.

"You broke my nose!"

The boy saw a girl with a bleeding fist. "Get out of here before I break your face!"

"Stupid bitch," Scott cursed. He pedaled past the girl, his two friends followed.

"You okay?" the girl asked. She helped him up. The boy nodded.

"What's your name?"

"Jake," he said.

"I'm Jess." She shook his hand. "You go to Oakland?"

Jake nodded.

"I'll see you there." Jess biked away.

"Thank you!" Jake yelled after her, but she already disappeared.

"Jake, you here?" Jess called from the door of the gas station.

"In the back!" a voice replied.

Jess headed into the station, past the shelves, and into the Employees Only room. She saw the three boys hunching over a computer screen.

"Play it again," Michael said. "And this time freeze where I tell you to."

Jess took a look at the footage. She saw Emma grabbing some things off the shelf.

"Okay, freeze."

The video stopped.

"What is that?" Michael squinted. "Why would she get so many? You said she only bought a coffee; you sure you got that receipt?"

Jake slammed a piece of paper onto the table. "You saw it like five times, dude."

"Are you saying she shoplifted? Emma would never do that."

"I'm not saying that, dude!"

"Okay, guys, let's stop staring at the freakin' screen and go out and see what's on that shelf," Rob said.

Michael leaped to the door, Jess moved out of the way, and Jake sprinted after him.

"What've you been up to?" Rob asked Jess.

She shrugged.

Michael and Jake headed to the shelf.

"No way!" Jake's eyes widened. "Dude, did you know about this?"

"What?" Jess walked over with Rob.

The four stared at the shelf. Stacks of boxes with the word "pregnancy test" held their attention.

Rob laughed. "You got your girl pregnant and now she left you. Typical."

"Don't say that," Jake warned. He looked at Michael. "Say something."

Michael looked at the box.

"It's a pregnancy test, if you still don't know wha—" Rob rolled his eyes.

"I know what it is!" Michael snapped. "Did any of you know about this? Did you?!"

"Calm down." Jake put his hand on Michael's shoulder.

"Get off me!" Michael pushed Jake back.

"Hey!" Jess yelled.

Michael threw the box on the floor and marched out the door.

"What is his problem?" Rob asked.

"Yeah, what is his problem?" Jake yelled. "His girlfriend is missing, and he just found out she's pregnant."

"Might be pregnant," Jess said. "If she used a bunch of these, then we should find them and take a look."

"Yeah, find them! As if they're lying around waiting for us," Jake complained.

"Hey!" Jess snapped him out of it. "I'm trying to help you here."

"Jake bit his lip. "You're right. I'm sorry."

"So, what now?" Rob cut in. "You're going to break into the Styles house?"

Jess paused for a moment. "Yeah…and you're gonna do it."

Jess grabbed Rob by the collar and walked him outside with Jake as he complained.

Jake saw Michael sitting on the curb. "You coming?"

"Where?"

"Come on."

Jake and Michael headed into Rob's car.

"Why are we taking my car?" Rob complained as Jess pushed him into the driver's seat.

"You ask a lot of questions." Jess cracked her knuckles. She sat in the passenger seat. "Come on, Michael, lead the way."

"What?"

"We're going to visit your girlfriend's place."

Rob drove for ten minutes and parked the car on the side of the street, meters away from the house.

"Get out," Jess told Rob.

"Why me?"

"Again, with the questions," Jess said. "Okay, listen up."

Michael and Jake straightened their backs. She told them the plan and all four headed out of the car.

Jake and Michael headed to the front door, while Jess and Rob went behind the house. The doorbell rang.

Jess and Rob crept into the backyard and waited by the kitchen door. They saw Michael and Jake talk to the Styles at the front door.

"You have the guts to show your face here at my door?" Mr. Styles growled.

"Mr. Styles, I'm here to apologize," Michael said. "I won't take too much of your time. Can I come in?"

Mr. Styles looked at Michael, then Jake. "Honey, can you come here for a second?"

Mrs. Styles came down the stairs. When she saw the two boys, she stopped.

"Come on in." Mr. Styles gestured for them. He closed the door after them.

The Styles and the boys sat in the living room.

"Can I get some water?" Jake asked.

Mrs. Styles sighed and got up.

"I can do it, I know my way around," Jake suggested. "It was only last year when I was here for Emma's birthday. Besides, you two have got a lot to talk about."

Jake went into the kitchen; he looked back and then tip-toed to the kitchen door. He unlocked it and Jess and Rob snuck in.

Jake whispered to them and signalled them to go Emma's room.

He walked back into the living room and sat next to Michael.

"Nice house you got here," Jake said.

"Okay, Michael cut to the chase," Mr. Styles cut in.

"Uh, uh, Mr. Styles," Michael began. Jess tip-toed behind the Styles and made it to the other side of the living room wall. She signalled for Rob to come.

Mr. Styles looked back, seeing the coast was clear.

"First, let me say," Michael continued. "That I'm really sorry. I'm so, so, so...."

Rob crossed to the other side and dropped his hat behind him.

"So, so, so."

Jess gestured for Rob to go back. He spread his hands out and mouthed "what?"

Jess shook her head and grabbed Rob by the hand. They crept up the stairs. Jess shrugged her shoulders at Michael as they went out of sight.

"So sorry," Michael finished. "You were right. I had no right to spread news about your daughter like that."

"He was being stupid," Jake added.

"I was being stupid, and it won't happen again."

"Is that all?" Mr. Styles rubbed his knees.

"No," Michael cut in. "I mean I still have so much to talk about," Michael gave a nervous laugh. "Isn't that right, Jake?"

"Yeah, like that time you broke Mr. Styles' window—"

Michael shook his head.

"And you fixed it later," Jake correct himself.

Michael still shook his head.

"Or not," Jake finished.

"Mr. Styles, I was just worried about your daughter," Michael said. "Did she call you yet? From her aunt's?"

"As a matter of fact, she did," Mrs. Styles cut in.

"Lila," Mr. Styles hissed.

"It's okay, honey, this will convince him to move on," Mrs. Styles assured.

"Really?" Michael asked in disbelief. "What did she say?"

"Michael, Emma needed some time away--"

"Away from what?"

"From you."

Jake swayed back, mouthing "woah."

"Lila," Mr. Styles hissed.

Upstairs, Jess and Rob searched through Emma's room. They found her closet turned inside out.

"She looks like she packed a bag in a hurry," Jess commented.

"It would take us forever to find anything here," Rob complained, plugging his nose. "It smells like shit too."

Jess looked under the bed, uncovered the sheets, and searched in the open drawers. "Yup, she definitely packed a bag."

"I think I'm going to vomit."

Jess grasped Rob's shoulders. "Get your shit together. Let's find the bathroom."

They headed out of Emma's room.

"She did runaway," Mrs. Styles' voice echoed from downstairs. Jess and Rob paused.

"She ran away from you."

Jess and Rob looked at each other in silence.

"Come on," Jess whispered. They headed into the washroom next to Emma's room. Jess searched the bin. Rob opened the cupboards under the sink.

"Found it," Jess pulled her hand out of the bin. She held a pregnancy test in hand.

"Ew." Rob shut his eyes in disgust.

Jess examined it and froze. "Geez."

"I think it's time you boys left," Mr. Styles' voice came from downstairs.

Jess and Rob headed to the stairs and saw the Styles showing the boys out. They stepped back and froze.

Michael and Jake saw their friends above and froze.

Mr. Styles opened the door. "I appreciate you coming here and taking the time to apologize, but it's just not going to work."

"Mr. Styles please let me explain," Michael urged as he stepped back out the door.

"Yeah, Mr. Styles," Jake added. "I mean is that a mole infestation you got over there." He pointed to the yard.

"What?" Mr. Styles stuck his head out the door.

Jess and Rob tip-toed down.

"I don't know what you're up to," Mr. Styles warned, stepping back in.

Jess and Rob ran up again.

"Don't come here again!" He shut the door.

"We're so dead," Jake said on the porch.

"Not yet," Michael went down to the driveway. "You hear that?" A rustle in the bushes lead Michael to the side of the house.

"Michael," a voice whispered.

"Rob?" Michael pondered. "Is that you?"

Rob hung from the edge of the roof. "A little help," he groaned.

"Oh my God." Jake caught up to Michael. They ran to the side of the house.

"Just let go," Michael said with his hands up. "Jake will catch you."

"No way." Jake shook his head.

"You're taller."

Rob let go and fell on Jake. Jake let out a scream as they tumbled onto the grass.

"Shhhh," Michael hissed.

The door opened.

"Michael!" Mr. Styles voice came roaring down on them. The cha-chank sound of a gun alarmed them.

Jess climbed out the window and jumped off the roof. "Let's go!"

Mr. Styles stormed down the porch and the group ran to the car.

"Get back here!"

Rob fidgeted for the keys.

"Open the door!" Jake yelled. "He's coming! Oh my God. We're gonna die."

"Calm down!" Jess yelled.

"I got it!" Rob said just as Jess punched a hole in the window.

"Hey!"

"Get in!" Jess unlocked the door and got in the car. The rest followed. Rob put the keys into the car and reversed it as Mr. Styles tapped on Jake's window.

Jake screamed.

"Come out here!" he yelled.

"Yeah, as if I'd want to be out there with you!" Jake yelled back.

Mr. Styles aimed his hunting gun at the car.

"Just go!" Jake screamed into Rob's ear. Rob stepped on the gas and accelerated; Jake and Michael flew back into their seats, and Jess swayed from side to side.

"I knew you had it in you," she said.

Chapter 3

Rob drove onto the highway.

Jess tossed something behind her; it landed on Michael's lap. "We found one," she said.

Michael picked it up. It was the pregnancy test.

"Is it positive?" Jake asked.

"How should I know?" Michael replied.

"Pink is for positive, blue is for negative," Jess informed.

"How did you know that?" Jake asked. "It's not like you were pregnant before."

"Or was I?" Jess snickered.

Everyone stared at Jess, wide-eyed.

"It says on the box, you idiots." Jess folded her arms.

"What color is it, Michael?" Jake asked.

"Pink."

"Looks like you're gonna be a daddy," Jess said. Michael and the boys held their breath.

"Now, keep driving, Rob," Jess cut in. "We're going to your house."

Jake gaped at Rob. "Rob's house?"

"My house?" Rob said at the same time as Jake.

"The Styles know where Jake and Michael live," Jess explained. "I'm sure they're headed over there wondering why two other strangers broke into their house."

"But, they don't know where you live," Rob said to Jess.

"That's true. But trust me, you don't want to know where I live."

"Oh-kay." Rob took the next exit.

Rob drove downtown and parked his car on the shared driveway. The townhouse had three floors with a narrow staircase. Loud music played from inside.

"Just so you know, I live with like four, maybe five, housemates," Rob warned, turning off the car engine.

"Do you not even know who you live with?" Jake asked.

"No, dude," Rob replied. "I barely spend any time at home. I just come here to sleep. The rest of the day I'm at school."

Everyone followed Rob up the metal staircase. He searched under the mat for the key but turned up empty-handed. "Stupid, Vanessa. Open up!" Rob banged on the door.

No one could hear him over the music.

"She always does this," Rob grumbled. He picked up a stone from a potted plant, leaned over the rail of the porch and hit it against the window above.

The window opened, and a girl's head popped out. "What?!" she yelled.

"Open the damn door!" Rob yelled back. "And stop taking the keys!"

"Get your own keys!" Vanessa stomped down the stairs and swung the door open.

"You're such an annoying little –" she paused when she saw they had company. "Oh, I didn't know we were having guests over." Her hands reached for her shirt as she pulled it down to expose some cleavage. She pulled on her hair tie and shook her hair down. "Ahem, where are my manners. Come in."

Rob rolled his eyes.

"I'm Vanessa," she stretched her hand out to Jake.

Jake turned red. "I'm Jake," he smiled.

"I'm Jess." Jess shook Vanessa's hand before Jake could. "Nice to meet you. Now we got a lot of work to do. If you can excuse us."

Rob took the boys up the stairs.

"Oh, cool." Vanessa followed. "What kind of work? Anything I can help with?"

Heavy metal music started to play upstairs.

"You like listening to people screaming?" Jake asked.

"Oh, no. That's just some random playlist I clicked on; I don't listen to that. I mean, do you?" Vanessa chatted behind Jake as they headed up.

"Sometimes."

"Really?" Vanessa beamed.

"Actually, it's all he listens to," Michael added.

"Oh my God," Vanessa squealed.

Rob squinted in distress.

"It's my favorite, too. I just didn't want to say anything, you know, 'cause I didn't want you to think I'm weird, but it's so weird that we both like the same music!" Vanessa went on.

Jake looked at Rob and mouthed, "She's so hot."

"Ew." Rob shook his head. "My room's this way."

They headed down the hall and into Rob's room. Vanessa was the last one.

"No," Rob said to her. "Don't you have something better to do?"

"I think I dropped my brush here somewhere?" Vanessa pointed under the bed.

"Nice try." Rob closed the door. "And turn off that horrible shit."

"If you need anything, let me know," Vanessa's voice called from behind the door. "I'm just next door."

"God, she's so annoying," Rob exhaled.

"Are you kidding? How did you never mention that you live with a hot chic?" Jake enunciated. "You have to hook me up."

"Trust me, you do not want to be with that monster." Rob rubbed his head.

"Oh? I didn't know she was your girl before; chill."

"That's not what happened, Jake," Rob roared. "Just back off, okay?"

"Geez, you really do have a thing for her since she did lose that brush here in your room."

"There is no brush, Jake!" Rob sat on his bed. "Oh my God. This was a bad idea. Why did we come here again?"

Jess took a look around Rob's room. Single bed, carpeted floor, and a neatly set-up desk. "Wow, it doesn't seem like you have much here."

"It's not like I'm gonna live here long," Jake brought his lips close to the wall. "Not with that crazy freak around."

"Hey!" Vanessa's voice came in from the other side.

Michael put the pregnancy test on the desk and slumped into a chair. "I was right."

"What?" Jake said to Michael. "You knew the whole time?"

"I had my suspicions. After all, her last words to me were, 'I need to tell you something important, promise not to freak out,'" Michael enunciated.

"So, just because a girl tells you that and takes off, you assumed she was pregnant?" Jess grinned.

"That and because, you know …" Michael paused. "three months ago, before our last fight, we…uh…did…" Jake made a circle with one hand and put a finger inside.

"Okay, I get it." Jess turned away. "You don't have to explain."

"Do you think that's why she ran away?" Jake asked.

"Maybe she got freaked out, and ran," Rob added. "You know, she needed some time and space, like what her mom said, she needed to get away from you for some time."

"If she did want that, I wouldn't have been the last person she saw," Michael said.

"You never really got to explain exactly what happened," Rob said. "What did she say to you?"

***

Michael thought of the time when he was on his way home from college. He had waited over an hour for Emma to come to the parking lot where they usually left together. Her class ended a while back and she still didn't show up.

"Emma, where are you?" Michael called her on her phone. He heard her panting on the other side.

"What do you mean by panting?" Jake asked, as Michael retold the story.

"Like she was running or scared, I don't know," Michael continued.

"I can't—" Emma answered the phone. Her voice had cut in and out.

"What?" Michael said. "I can't hear you."

"Meet me at the truss bridge," she said.

Then, the phone went static. Michael got in the car and drove away from the college parking lot.

He headed past the houses and down a hill. He parked his car at a dead-end road. He grabbed his phone, seeing as the sun was setting and it would be dark soon.

He lit his path down through the trail among the bushes. Once he got down to the hill, he made his way over the bridge.

"Emma?!" he yelled.

"Over here," a voice called back. He saw a phone light flash ahead under the bridge.

When Michael was a few meters away, Emma ran toward him. She hugged him tightly.

"Woah, woah, take it easy," he said, staggering back.

"I'm so glad you could make it." Emma sighed. "I missed you so much."

"Missed me?" Michael looked at Emma's wet face. "Were you crying?"

"No, no, it's just water."

Michael saw that Emma was drenched. "Oh my God, are you okay? Where were you?"

"I can't talk too long now," she said, looking back.

"Where's your car? How did you get here?"

"Look, I can't explain, we're running out of time. I just wanted to see you before … before…."

"Before what? Slow down."

"You have been the best friend and boyfriend any one could have," Emma continued. "I wanted you to know that, and it will still be like that, no matter what happens."

Emma's phone rang. "Oh no." She jumped. "I have to go."

Michael grabbed Emma by the shoulders. "What is going on? Where are you going?"

"I will be back soon, I promise." Emma kissed Michael. She ran ahead, under the bridge and around the corner.

"Emma, wait!"

"I'll be back," she called over her shoulder. "I'll be back!"

***

"Hmm…" Jess rested the side of her head on her hand. She sat on the opposite side of the bed from Rob, while Jake paced back and forth to think.

"So, clearly, she was running away from something," Jake said. "She did get a phone call before she left, right?"

"Yeah, this sounds a lot like what happened in class," Rob said. "She checked her phone and bolted out of the room with all her things."

"You think she saw the doc at school?" Jess added. "She did grab a lot of pregnancy tests and headed to class after that."

"There would be a one-hour break before she came to class," Rob said. "She could've gone to the school clinic before getting there."

"Okay, Rob, go talk to the doc tomorrow," Jess said. "If Emma left school right after she checked her phone in class, that's probably when she headed home to pack her stuff. I only found one pregnancy test in her bathroom, so it would make sense for the rest to be at school."

"I'm not going through the school's garbage," said Rob.

"We don't have to. We already know that Emma's pregnant." Jake rolled his eyes.

"Good," Rob concluded.

"What do you mean, good?" Michael cut in. "My girlfriend is missing and pregnant, and I'm going to be a dad!"

Silence filled the room.

"If Emma really did go to the school doc," Rob added after a few moments. "I think I know a way to get what we need."

Rob knocked on Vanessa's door.

"What?" Vanessa swung the door open. She quickly had done a new makeover and wore a tank top with black tights.

"We need your help."

She slammed the door shut.

"Come on," Rob knocked hard.

"Vanessa," Jake stepped in. "It's me, Jake, can I come in? Just me?"

Vanessa opened the door with a smile.

Jake went in. He turned around to give everyone the thumbs up. "Wish me luck," he mouthed.

Michael, Jess and Rob sat on Rob's bed, waiting.

Michael sighed.

"What's taking him so long?" Michael complained.

"It's Vanessa," Rob mumbled.

Jess, sitting on the end of the bed, squeezed the sheets in her hands. "I can't believe him."

"You okay?" Michael asked, lying down next to Rob. "I mean, you and Jake go way back, right? I'm sure he's just talking to her."

Rob grunted. Michael nudged him to shut up.

"How'd you two meet, anyway?" Rob added. "Considering since you're both the same age, like four years older than us."

"I can't wait anymore." Jess got up. She walked over to Vanessa's room and before knocking on the door, it opened.

"Jess," Jake said, his face red.

"You forgot to thank me," Vanessa said from behind.

Jake turned around. "Than—"

Vanessa's lips closed around his.

"Woah, okay," he paused. "Thanks?" He turned to find that Jess was gone. "Where'd she go?"

Vanessa shrugged.

Jake went after Jess.

"Where are you going?" Michael stood in his way.

"Stay here," Jake said. "Emma's parents could still be out looking for you." Jake disappeared down the stairs.

"And you!" Michael yelled after him. They're looking for you too!" But, Jake had already gotten out the door.

"Come on," Rob motioned for Michael to come back into his room. "I got a sleeping bag."

"Jess!" Jake called on the street. "Come back here! You know I didn't mean for that to happen. Jess!"

Jake remembered a time when a girl asked him to the Prom dance. Jess wouldn't talk to him for days, even though he hadn't even given the girl an answer yet. He was biking home and he knew where to find Jess.

He biked down a street and into a park trail. He found Jess sitting on the handrail on the end of the trail.

"Jess!" He braked.

"Go away!" Jess got on her bike to leave.

"Wait, I just want to talk!"

Jess pedalled away, and Jake caught up to her, bringing his bike in Jess' way.

"Stop!"

Jess braked.

"Why are you so upset?"

"Why am I so upset?" Jess gasped for air. "I can't believe you! After all these years."

Tears ran down Jess' eyes. He had never seen her cry.

Now, Jake found Jess sitting at the bus stop and wiping her tears.

"Hey," Jake said gently. He took a seat next to Jess. Jess wiped her face and looked away.

"This is the second time I've seen you like this," Jake said. "Remember the first time?"

Jess nodded after a minute. A pendant on a chain dangled in front of her. Jess gasped. She clasped it close to her heart. "You still have it?"

"Yup," Jake nodded. "I always wear it around my neck."

Jess looked at Jake and punched him on the shoulder.

"Oww."

"You had my pendant this whole time and you didn't tell me?"

"You're the one who threw it at me. I thought you didn't want it anymore."

"I do."

"Keep it. I gave it to you a long time ago, and I meant what I'd said."

Jess turned red. "Okay." The bus arrived.

"You sure you don't want to stay with us?"

"I won't be far." Jess got on the bus. She popped her head back out. "And Jake?"

"Mmm?"

"Thank you."

Chapter 4

"**O**kay, guys, you're gonna have to give me some space," Vanessa said. She instructed Rob, Michael, and Jake to stay hidden behind a wall as she walked into the health clinic in the basement level of Oakland College.

Vanessa pulled on her badge and swiped it at the back door. She wore a volunteer shirt.

"How'd you know Vanessa was part of the health club?" Jake asked.

"I just guessed," Rob said. "She's the only person I know whose part of every club at school. She just wants everyone to know who she is; I can't believe Michael never met her."

"I'm hardly in school, man," Michael said. "I only started going to my classes again, so I could have an excuse to pick up Emma on the way home."

"Don't worry." Jake put a hand on Michael's shoulder. "We'll find her soon."

Vanessa stepped back out.

"Did you find anything?" Rob asked.

"Calm down, tiger," she purred.

Rob took a step back in disgust.

"You can't handle this." Vanessa took her phone out from under her shirt.

"Why would you do that?" Rob covered his eyes.

"In case they wanted to search me."

"Why would the doctor want to search you?"

"I don't know, Rob," Vanessa enunciated. "What else would a doctor do?"

"Can we just get out of here?" Michael shuddered. "Like now?"

Vanessa wrapped an arm around Jake's. She unlocked her phone and it opened up to show a picture of her half-naked. "Oops, sorry, wrong one." She giggled. "Here it is."

Michael snatched the phone.

"Hey!" Vanessa tried to get it back from him.

Michael zoomed in to see Emma's name on the check-in list. "Jess was right! Emma did come here."

"There's more," Vanessa swiped a finger across her phone screen. "She did a urine test. It was in her file. She's pregnant. I guess she checked her email in class."

Michael's jaw dropped. "She's two months pregnant?"

"Was that around the same time you, you know…fire in the hole?" Jake asked.

"Seriously?" Rob mocked.

"I like the way you think," Vanessa smiled.

Michael covered his face and headed to the first exit.

"She probably went to get an abortion." Vanessa took her phone back. "Maybe that's why she didn't tell you. She didn't want you to know, because she knew you'd still want to be the daddy."

Michael froze.

"Oh shit, I was right." Vanessa popped a piece of bubble gum in her mouth.

"That does sound like something Emma would do," Jake nodded.

"You think her parents know?" Rob asked. "Maybe that's why they're keeping it all under cover?"

Michael felt a tap on his shoulder and turned.

"Mr. Danes," a man with glasses stood with his arms folded.

"Chris … I mean Professor," Michael held his hands up. "I'm not here to hang posters."

"Yeah, I know you're not here to hang posters, because you went to the paper!" Chris held up the newspaper. Emma's marathon picture was on the front page.

Jake laughed. "Wow, she really did it."

"You better come with me." Chris grabbed Michael's arm.

"Let him go," a voice interrupted.

Everyone turned to see an officer from the neighborhood's precinct.

"Officer Steve," Chris smirked. "Arrest this boy."

"This boy," Officer Steve walked over to Michael, "was right."

"What?" Chris said at the same time as the others.

"The aunt called yesterday. Emma was a no-show," Officer Steve explained. "We got a call from someone on the highway, said they found something. I need you all, except you Chris, to come down to the precinct with me."

"Is it Emma? Did they find her?" Michael asked.

"You'll see when we get there."

"This is not over, Mr. Danes," Chris enunciated. "I want you back here immediately when this is all," Chris gestured to the group, "sorted."

"Take it down a notch, Chris," Steve inhaled into Chris' face.

Chris squinted from Steve's bad breath.

"This one's on me. Stop hassling the kid. He was doing his job, which you miserably failed at."

"Ohhhh … snap …" Jake mouthed.

"Do I have to go?" Vanessa asked.

Rob covered her mouth. "She means yes," he corrected, "she would love to help."

"Why'd you do that?" she whispered to Rob as they all headed up the stairs past Chris.

"And here I thought you were smart," Rob snickered. "You have Emma's file."

"Oh my God, you are so dead," Vanessa whispered. "The doc is going to kill me."

"Don't say bye to your MCAT just yet," Rob whispered.

At the precinct, Steve showed the kids into the lab.

"I thought nothing ever happens here," Vanessa whispered.

Rob snorted. "Not everything revolves around you."

Vanessa pushed him away.

"Hey, hey," Steve scolded. He tossed them all gloves to wear. "Is there anyone else I should know about at school who Emma hangs out with?"

"Rob?" Michael looked at him.

"Emma and I are in the same program, I hardly ever see her talk to anyone in class," Rob explained.

"Yeah, she's more of an introvert, I'd say," Jake added. "Are we under investigation?"

"No one is under investigation just yet," Steve assured. He stood in front of an evidence bag on the table.

Michael and the rest gathered around.

Steve, with blue gloves on, unzipped the bag. "Look familiar?" He held a pink sweater with a drop of blood on its sleeve.

Jake shrugged his shoulders.

"I don't know," Rob shook his head.

"Michael?" Steve asked.

"Yeah." Michael held his breath. "That's what she was wearing when I last saw her."

Chapter 5

"Susan," Steve yelled to the back of the lab. "Get me the Styles."

Michael and his friends sat in the hallway, waiting. Jake was falling asleep on Rob's shoulder when Emma's parents walked in.

"What's the matter, Officer?" Mrs. Styles asked. She had a winter coat on, but still shivered.

"Steve?" Mr. Styles asked when he saw Michael and his friends waiting in front of the lab.

From the lab door window, Mrs. Styles saw her daughter's sweater on the table. "No…." She walked in, held the blood-stained sleeve and brought it closer to her face. "My baby…."

"Mrs. Styles, I need you to put that down," Steve said. "It's evidence."

"What?" Mrs. Styles turned red which matched her blood-shot eyes.

"What evidence?!" Mr. Styles roared. "I thought we had come to an agreement." He looked at the boys.

Steve stood between the boys and Emma's father. He put his hands up to get Steve to back up.

"The boys had nothing to do with it," Steve assured him. "Someone on the highway reported seeing this sweater."

"What highway?"

"Highway 64," Steve said. "Going East."

"What?" Mr. Styles' eyes widened. "Why would she go there?"

"You tell me." Steve folded his arms. "She's supposed to be heading south, and yet here we are…with a blood-stained sweater."

Mrs. Styles sobbed.

"How do we know it's her blood?" Mr. Styles asked.

"We'll need a hair sample," Steve explained. "To get a match."

"No need," Vanessa interrupted, scrolling through her phone. "I have her file."

"Who are…who is this girl?" Mr. Styles argued. "How do you know my daughter?"

Steve held Mr. Styles back. "You need to calm down or I'm gonna have to ask you to leave."

"Send that file to the lab," Steve instructed, tossing her a card with an email. He turned to look at the Styles. "Now, is there anything you're not telling me?"

"Oh, no," Mrs. Styles wept.

Steve grabbed her shoulder and sat her down in a chair.

"We didn't know what to do."

"About what?" Steve said.

"Maybe we shouldn't say anything until we get a lawyer here," Mr. Styles paced, taking his phone out of his pocket.

"Just sit down," Steve demanded.

Mr. Styles froze and did what he was told. "Do we really need them to be here?" he inquired.

"It's okay, hon," Mrs. Styles added. "They're her friends too. It's time you all learned the truth."

***

A week ago, Mrs. Styles carried a laundry basket down the hall. She went into Emma's bedroom. "Honey?"

She searched the bedroom, but Emma wasn't there. On the other side of the bedroom wall, she heard crying.

"Emma?" Mrs. Styles knocked on the door.

Emma, sitting on the toilet and crying, held her breath.

"Are you crying?"

Emma tossed the pregnancy test into the bin, pulled up her pants and flushed the toilet.

"Can I come in?"

"In a minute," Emma replied. She let the water run from the tap, as she washed her face and smudged eyes. She took her eyeliner out of the drawer and some foundation and redid her makeup.

"Emma?"

"Yes?" Emma opened the door.

"Are you okay?" Mrs. Styles put her hands on Emma's shoulders. "I thought I heard crying. Is it Michael again?"

Emma sighed.

Mrs. Styles hugged her. "That boy is just trouble. You know it would make your dad happy if you had just moved on."

"Mom," Emma groaned. "We did not break up, and we never will. Just stop it with the act!"

"What act?"

Emma barged past her mom and into her room. "You're the one who would be happy if we broke up. Leave Dad out of this."

Something caught Mrs. Styles' attention as she walked into the bathroom. She covered her mouth. "No!" She walked into Emma's room to find her packing. "You're pregnant?!"

Emma ignored her mom. She shoved pants and sweaters into her bag.

"What are you doing?"

"I'm going away."

"Honey, I'm home." Mr. Styles walked into the house with bags of groceries.

"Just wait until your dad hears about this," Mrs. Styles said as she headed down the stairs.

"No, wait, please." Emma rushed after her.

"What's going on?" Mr. Styles said from the door. Both women paused on the stairs.

"Our daughter is pregnant!"

Bags of fruits and vegetables fell from Mr. Styles' hands. He went to grab his hunting gun. "I'll show that Danes boy."

"Dad!" Emma held onto the rifle. "Please, stop!"

"Let go of the gun," Mrs. Styles uttered with tears in her eyes.

"He doesn't know!" Emma continued. "I don't want him to know."

"Well, I'll tell him." Mr. Styles pulled on the rifle. "He'll answer to my gun for ruining my girl's life."

"I'm going to get rid of it!" Emma shut her eyes.

"What?" Her father froze in his footsteps.

Emma's mom sat on the bottom step and cried.

"I'm going to get rid of it," she said. "I'll get an abortion." She paused "If you tell him, he'll want to keep it. That's why we have to keep this a secret. Now, put the gun down."

***

"I called my sister," Mr. Styles explained to everyone in the lab. "We decided she would take care of her while the operation was done in Florida. Emma left that same day."

"What time?" Michael asked.

Mr. Styles shook his head.

"What time?!"

"Around four?" Mr. Styles looked at his wife.

"That's when I was waiting for Emma in the parking lot," Michael went on. "When she called me."

"She called you?" Mr. Styles gawked.

"She wanted to meet me."

"I don't understand," Mr. Styles mumbled. His wife cried even more while at his side.

"We met under the truss bridge," Michael added.

"Which is on highway 64," Jake continued.

"And she was wearing this sweater. It was wet!" Michael felt the sweater, but it was dry. "it must have been laying on the ground for days."

"So, you think, the sweater's been on the ground since the day she disappeared, when you last saw her?" Steve asked, writing in his notepad.

Michael nodded. "She was drenched, completely, like she had fallen into a lake. She also smelled weird."

"Like what?" Steve said.

"Like Jake's gas station."

Steve smelled the sweater. "Petrol." He looked at Jake. "Jake, were you working at the station that night?"

Jake shook his head.

"Get me on the phone with your manager."

"Okay, I have to go," Vanessa said. "Everything is in the email. I'll have to talk to the doc about faxing you the rest of the files, anything that might help with the case." Vanessa walked out. Rob followed her.

"Hey, I know I don't usually say this," Rob said.

"Is this going to turn into a love confession?" Vanessa chewed her gum loudly. "Because I know you love me."

"Oh wow, Rob groaned. "Will you just listen to yourself? I'm trying to thank you here."

"Oh," Vanessa froze. "Don't thank me. I can't wait until I get my name in the paper. Vanessa Hodge, soon-to-be doctor, aided in the search for Oakland's missing girl. It's going to be great for my MCAT interview!" Vanessa headed out the precinct.

Rob shook his head. He saw a group of reporters and camera men gather around outside.

"Guys? We got company."

Jake popped his head out from the lab. "Are we gonna be on TV?"

"Susan, keep them out of my building," Steve yelled from the door. "Becky, you copy?" He spoke into his radio receiver. "I need you and Don back here. We got some paparazzi trouble."

"On it," a voice said from Steve's radio.

"I need to get an APB on Emma's location, if she's still using her car, I need her plate number, license, birth certificate and any other ID that can identify her. Does she have like a birthmark or scar?" Steve asked Emma's parents.

"W-why?" Mrs. Styles held her breath. "You think she's dead?"

"We have to look at all our options here," Steve said, putting the sweater back into the evidence bag. He picked up his phone and made a call. "I need you in the lab, now." Steve saw Michael about to leave. "Stay," he said, looking back at Emma's parents as he continued to talk on the phone.

Michael looked at Rob and Jake. "You guys go. I'll sit here with Emma's parents."

"Yeah, I got school, man," Rob said. "I'll come by your place tomorrow."

"Oh, shit, I forgot to call my mom," Michael muttered.

"I talked to her last night. She kept calling you on your phone while you were asleep." Rob smiled.

"Thanks, man." Michael hugged his friend.

"Okay." Rob held his hands up. "Gotta go." Rob ran out the door and past the reporters.

"I have to go meet with my manager," Jake explained. "He's got a lot of questions about what's happening."

"It's okay, go."

"You sure?"

Michael nodded. He went back in the lab.

"Michael, I'm going to need a finger printing analysis done," Steve explained. "I need you to roll up your sleeves and put your hands here, you know it's just to get your name out of the way."

Michael took a seat and got his hands scanned.

"I'm going to need you and Mrs. Styles' fingerprints as well. In case we find Emma and need to identify any prints on her."

Mrs. Styles cried.

"Don't worry," Michael assured. "Emma's strong. She'll be back like she promised."

***

A trunk opened, revealing a girl curled up and with closed eyes.

"Wake up!" A voice yelled as water splashed onto the girl's face.

The girl gasped. She grabbed the water bottle and drank. "Where are we?"

"You don't get to ask the questions here," a voice said behind a mask. "Now get up."

The girl hesitated, and the man reached for her arm and pulled her out. They were in a forest, surrounded by tall trees with no civilization or human in sight.

The man tied a rope to the tape around the girl's wrists. "Walk." He pushed her.

"Are you going to kill me?" she inquired. "Bury me here where no one can ever know?"

"You know, for a Robertson girl, I thought you'd be smarter than that."

"You don't have to hide your face," the girl added, walking in front of the man. "I know who you are."

The man pushed the girl against a tree, removed his mask, and stared her in the eyes.

She saw burn marks on his forehead. He covered it well with his greying black hair, half tied into a pony tail.

"Do you?" the man hissed. He breathed heavily into the girl's face. Wrinkles and sagging eye bags circled the man's gaping blue eyes. She could see her reflection in them. She shut her eyes. "That's what I thought. Now, keep moving."

Chapter 6

"Hi, is this Ava?"

"Speaking," a voice answered.

"My name is Michael," the other voice replied.

"Yes? I know who you are, Michael. Now, why are you calling me?"

Michael exhaled in relief. "I thought I might have to start from the beginning, but this is good. I mean, that I can just cut right to the chase. When did you last speak with Emma?"

"Excuse me? Michael, what makes you think I'm at any liberty to speak with you? For all I know, you could be keeping Emma somewhere, not wanting her to have an abortion. Who knows, you might even keep her there until she gives birth, so you can have your baby, and the family money, assuming you know our history."

"What?" Michael's jaw dropped. "This is not about money! I don't even know what family history you're talking about. I don't know where Emma is, and I'm certainly not keeping her anywhere. If I knew where she was, I wouldn't be calling and going through all the effort of trying to find her."

"Who knows? It could be all a charade. I don't know why Tommy let her hang out with you. Don't call me again, Michael."

Ava hung up. She stood in front of a Van Gogh painting; its glass reflected a three-tier chandelier hanging in the center of a grand entrance with a spiral staircase. Vanilla cream marble tiled the floors supporting ionic columns that stretched up to the roof, a part of it embraced by a central dome. Between hunting pieces, a mahogany grandfather clock struck three. Ava clicked her heels as she walked up the spiral staircase and into a library. Greek and Roman Classics in their original form procured by some collector, were arranged in two rooms with entrances of thirty feet high. Maps, trophies, and awards covered the walls. Pictures of Tommy and Ava revealed them to be shaking hands with a construction builder. Other pictures showed Ava and Tommy holding a big-sized check from a mayor. Ava paused to look at a framed certificate that said: award for excellence in the Robertson pipeline expansion.

"You know we signed memorandums with six contractors for expanding this pipeline," Ava said. "Seven point four million dollars was spent on each contract. Do you know how much money that is?" Ava turned to look at a man tied to his chair. He had a rag in his mouth as he tried to shake it out.

Ava nodded, and another man removed the rag from the man's mouth.

"Now, tell me, where is she?"

                              ***

"God, I never knew Emma's aunt could be such a bitch,"
Michael sighed. "Well, that didn't get us anywhere."

"Relax, Michael," Jake said from the gas station counter.

Michael handed the phone back to Jake.

"The cops are taking care of it. I'm sure they talked to
Emma's aunt already."

"Did you hear what she said? Family history, money, what
was that all about?"

"You think Emma's family is rich or something?"

"They lived in a rundown house for almost a decade, Jake,
so no I don't think they're rich. You know the number of times
I had to loan Emma money for school? She was taking on two
jobs. If the family had any money, Emma wouldn't have had to
work so hard. I loaned her the money just so I could even get to
see her, man."

"Maybe, it's just the aunt who's rich."

"Who leaves out a rich aunt in a conversation? I just heard
the name Ava for the first time. I thought the whole story about
the aunt in Florida was a lie. Now, that there really is an aunt, I
wonder if Emma was really going there to get an abortion
without telling me. She did say she'd be back, maybe she
meant after the abortion."

"Beer?" Jake put a can on the counter.

"No!" Michael raged.

"It's on me."

Michael took the beer and drank.

"Man, you've been going crazy since that video," Jake said. "Who buys a gallon of petrol and dumps it on themselves?"

"Well, why don't we ask Emma when she comes back?" Michael laughed hysterically. "Maybe then we'll realize that I'm not the one who's crazy." Michael went to the fridge and took out another beer.

"Hey, hey," Jake peeped over the counter. "I did say one free beer."

Michael drank it all. "She's carrying my child. I have a right to know where she is. I'm not just some man she could manipulate and do with whatever she wants."

Michael drank another one and then another one as he sat on the floor, his back to the fridge. "You know what? S-screw her. She lied to me; she lied to my face, and I'm the one still chasing after her."

"Oh, dude," Jake looked at a number of empty beer cans. "I just got this job."

***

"What is the last known location of Emma's phone?" Steve asked over his desk. A number of cops had been digging into the case of Emma Styles, making phone calls one after the other. "And, I'm still waiting for that APB!"

A lab technician walked into Steve's office. "It's a match," he said.

"The blood on the sweater's a match to Emma Styles?"

"Not Emma Styles," the lab technician gestured for Steve to come with him.

In the lab, the technician showed Steve the computer screen.

"I ran her blood into the system, and this popped up."

Steve saw a picture of a young Emma and her parents in front of a building. The sign read Roberston.

"Tell me," Steve said, sitting in the Styles' home, "why I have a picture of the Robertsons with your faces on it?"

"We can explain, Mr. Styles said.

"Save me the bullshit, Tom, or should I say Tommy Robertson. Who are you people? You walk into my town, live among us for almost ten years, and call yourselves the Styles?"

Steve pulled a wallet from his jacket pocket.

"That's my—"

"I had to be sure, Tom," Steve said, taking out a business card from the wallet. He put it on the table. Tommy Robertson was written in the middle of it.

"Okay, let me explain."

***

"Emma!" Michael and Jake called on the highway. Beeping cars flew past them. "Emma!"

They searched the road in their drunkenly state and headed onto the truss bridge.

"Emma!" Michael's voice echoed over a small dried up ravine. "Aw man, I really screwed up."

"It's not your fault," Jake slapped Michael's face. "Wake up."

"We had a big fight… again… two months ago," Michael said as he leaned over the bridge. "I thought we worked through it…especially since she started talking to me again. Now, I know it was all a lie. I fell for a girl who broke my heart."

A beeping car whooshed past them. Michael almost fell over the bridge, but Jake caught him.

"Woah, man, we should head back."

Through the wire fence of the bridge, Michael pointed toward the ravine.

"I know; I know that was where you last saw Emma."

"Car."

"Car?" Jake looked over the bridge and saw a car slanted down the forested hill. "Car."

Jake shook Michael. "We found Emma's car!" He kissed him on the forehead.

Michael threw up.

Jake helped Michael down the hill. The sky had turned a dark blue. Soon they wouldn't be able to see anything. They reached Emma's car, its trunk was open. Jake stepped on a small bundle of metal. The car beeped once as the back lights turned red. He turned on his phone and lit up the ground to find car keys. "There's blood on them."

"Don't touch them," the pale Michael said. "Just take a picture and use your sleeve to open the door."

Jake pointed his phone light through the windows. "Aw man, this is not good."

Michael peeked through the window to find Emma's bags opened.

Jake pulled his sleeve down and touched the door handle.

"Step away from the car," a voice interrupted. The boys turned around to see that it was Steve with a flashlight. They saw red and blue blinking lights of a police car from the bridge.

"How'd you find us?" Jake asked.

Michael puked again.

"You okay there?" Steve approached the boys. "Go home, son." He tapped Michael on the shoulder. "We got this." Steve looked behind him at the forensics team and a few officers. "Bag everything."

"Is she in there?" Michael said, wiping his mouth. "Is she dead?"

"We found footprints," one officer said, pointing a flashlight into the forest.

"I should look for her." Michael straightened his back and swayed.

"Not in that state. Jake, take him home."

"Yes, sir." Jake helped Michael up and they walked back up the hill.

***

The girl vomited into a bush by a fire.

"That's the third time today," said the man with the burnt scars. "You seemed quite fine when I first met you. Except for that stench of petrol. Did you really think you could do it--kill yourself?"

"If that's what it'd take to stop you." The girl shivered by the fire.

"Sweetheart," the man smiled. "I would have still gotten what I wanted."

"Not if I was dead." The girl spat mucus onto the ground. "You would get nothing."

The man spun a rabbit on a skewer above the flames. "I could still get my money, whether you're alive or not. No one would have to know until after I got what I came for. That was the deal after all."

"So, why keep me alive then?"

"Because, you are so much like your mother."

***

Steve bagged Emma's cell phone. He found the car keys in the ignition.

"She seems to have left the car running until the fuel went out," Steve said to an officer. "Now, why would she do that if she wasn't coming back?"

"Sir, all the bags seemed to have been searched and dumped out in the back," the officer replied from the backseat. "We won't be able to tell what's missing unless we bring it back to evidence and get the parents to look at it."

"Okay, meet me back at the precinct and call them in. Nice work, Becky." Steve gave the bagged phone to Officer Becky. He pointed his flashlight onto the footprints in the mud and grabbed one of Emma's shoes from the backseat. "Don, you back here?"

Steve bent down to measure the length of the print. The boot print was almost as long as his boot. "If I remember correctly, Becky's only five-foot six. And this is a size eight." Steve put Becky's shoe over the print. It was an inch smaller than the print.

"Looks like we got our guy."

Steve remembered what Mr. Styles said about the Robertsons.

"My sister is Ava Robertson," he explained in his house. "Ten years ago, I managed the New York Branch, while my sister worked as one of the partners for the Florida branch. I was to sign a contract with a contractor."

Mrs. Styles turned away. "Do we really have to go over this?"

"If it can help us find Emma, then we have to, honey," Mr. Styles comforted. "You see, Steve, I wasn't a very good husband. I had an affair with this female contractor, who ruined my life, my company and my family. We wanted Emma far from this, especially if word got out to the paper, which never did, and we hope to keep it that way. We didn't change our names, give up our life in New York, and move here for this."

"Give me her name," Steve scribbled into his note pad.

"Samantha Cooke," Mr. Styles said.

"Susan, did you find anything on Samantha Cooke?" Steve said into his radio. "Don?" Steve followed the footprints in the forest trail. They came to a halt on the other end of the highway.

"Skid marks," an officer said, crossing the road and meeting up with Steve. "Looks like our kidnapper hid his car over there and intercepted our girl back at the car location."

"Don, you think you can locate the type of car our kidnapper had?"

"Yes, sir."

"What do you think really happened?"

"I think Miss Styles got involved with some really bad people."

Steve headed back to the precinct and was ambushed by a group of reporters. He parked his car, took a deep breath, and kept his head down as he walked out.

"Officer Steve," one reporter intervened, shoving her microphone into Steve's face. "What can you tell us about Emma Styles? Was she found in her car?"

"Who told you that?" Steve snapped. "This is a confidential police case and I'm not at liberty to share anything with you. Anything you say or do may hinder our search and put Miss

Styles in danger. I suggest you stop publicizing false information immediately, if you care about saving this girl."

The reporter paused in silence.

"Does this mean Miss Styles is alive?" another reporter cut in. Steve pushed through the crowd and headed to the precinct door. He locked it behind him. "Geez, how long have they been here?"

"All day," Susan said from her desk. She handed Steve a file. "Got this shipped in today from the supreme court. I had to be on call with them all morning until they finally shoved that 'it's not within your jurisdiction' part up their ass. This is as much as we could get, the rest you have to get approval on from the feds."

"Wow, this Cooke woman must have really made herself known to the world." Steve rummaged through the big file as he walked over to his desk. He found two boxes in his work space. "Susan, how many more of these boxes do I have to go through?"

"There are two more coming tomorrow," Susan called over her back. "Hold please," she said as she hung up the phone. It rang again.

"Becky, did you run the phone history into the system?" Steve asked Becky at her desk. She had a framed photo of her with Jess, and a picture of herself and her son--with whom must have been the dad--crossed out.

"Still waiting to hear back from the phone company," she cupped the phone.

"And the Styles?"

"They're not answering."

Steve sighed as he swiveled in his chair and rubbed his head. He found a video of Emma, frozen on his screen. It showed Emma in the back of the gas station pouring petrol over herself. Steve kept rewinding the footage. He paused it every few seconds just before Emma poured the petrol on herself. "She keeps looking to her left," he mumbled. "Why?"

Steve's eyes widened. "She knew her kidnapper," he announced. Steve rushed over to Becky and grabbed Emma's charging phone. He discovered it was password protected when he tried to unlock it. He took out his phone and dialed a number.

***

"I'm sorry to have bothered you, Mrs. Danes," Jake said, barging into the door with Michael on his shoulders.

"Ever since Emma's been officially reported missing," Michael's mother said, grabbing Michael's other shoulder, "he stopped coming home. He doesn't answer his phone, and he doesn't tell me anything."

The two carried Michael over to the living room couch. A notebook fell from his jacket pocket. Mrs. Danes opened it.

"Oh, no, no, no, no, no …" Jake grabbed the note book and smiled. "This is Michael's diary."

"Give me that," Mrs. Danes pulled on it.

"I don't think Michael would want you to see this," Jake tugged at it.

"He's my son."

"He's my friend."

The notebook opened, and a picture of a young Emma, Michael, and the gang fell out. On the back of the picture was an inscription:

"To the bestest of friends I ever had. Thank you for making Oakland my home. E," Mrs. Danes read out loud. "Oh, Michael." She sat down on the floor.

With the book wide open, entries of Emma's case were written in detail. Each page was titled by the number of days since Emma had been missing. The latest entry showed a drawing of a baby in a girl's womb.

"No …" Mrs. Danes covered her mouth. "How did this happen?"

Jake closed the book and took the picture from her hand. "I'm sorry, Mrs. Danes."

"You knew?" She slapped Jake across the face.

"Oww," he screamed.

"Get out of my house!" Mrs. Danes yelled.

Jake stormed to the door. He opened it to leave, and Officer Steve stood in his way. He walked in.

"Mrs. Danes," he nodded and squinted at Michael on the couch. "Where are you going?" Steve held Jake back. "I need you here."

Jake covered his cheek.

"Geez, do I need to separate you two?" Steve shut the door behind him and shoved Jake into a seat on the other side of the room. "I'll take this." He took Michael's notebook. He saw the picture of the gang when they were young. Emma looked just like the Robertson girl Steve saw on his screen. He tucked it under the journal as he flipped through the pages.

"You've been running your own investigation this whole time?"

"No." Jake folded his arms.

"Mrs. Danes, I think you missed the other cheek." Steve looked at Michael's mom. She rolled up her sleeve.

"No, no, no, no, stop!" Jake held his hands up. "I'll tell you everything…everything I know."

Mrs. Danes made some coffee. She woke Michael up to drink some. Once he sobered up, Jake had finally finished talking.

"What happened?" Michael asked. "The car!"

"It's fine, Michael," Steve said. "It's taken care of. I'm not here for that. I need you to unlock this." Steve tossed a pair of gloves to Michael and gave him a phone.

"Emma's phone," Michael turned it on.

"Did Emma get into trouble with a bad guy?" Steve asked.

Michael shook his head. "She only ever hung out with me and sometimes the gang." Michael typed Emma's password, but it didn't work. "What?" He tried a couple of others but no luck.

"Looks like you didn't know your girl that well," Steve sighed.

"Did you try your name?" Jake said.

"She always uses Emma Rose as her password, because she loved roses," Michael said. "I can't believe this; when did she change it?"

"Try Robertson," Steve suggested.

"Who the hell is Robertson?" Jake asked.

"Just try it."

Michael typed it in and it worked. A chat box popped up from an unknown number. "Meet me at Highway 64, just past the Truss bridge," the text said. "Don't forget our deal. I bring you the money; you give me the originals."

Steve snatched the phone from Michael's hands.

"No, wait," Michael got out of the couch, still a bit woozy. "I can help! Please, I need to know what happened."

"Stay home!" Steve scolded and left the house. "And if you remember anything about who Emma might have gotten involved with, let me know!"

The door slammed shut and Jake got up slowly to leave.

"Wait," Michael urged.

"Aww man," Jake paused, took out his phone and tossed it to Michael.

Steve made the next stop at the Styles' house. The lights were out, and the car was gone.

"Mrs. Styles," he knocked on the door. "It's Steve. Open up. If you don't open this door, you're only going to look more suspicious. Daughter gets kidnapped and parents leave the city. Is that the kind of press you want?"

A light turned on and Mrs. Styles answered the door.

"I have nothing more to say to you, Steve," Mrs. Styles talked in a hoarse voice. Her eyes were red, and her face was swollen.

"Where's Tom?"

"Visiting some family in Florida."

"In Florida?" Steve held the door with his hand before Mrs. Styles could close it. "I'm going to need an address."

"My husband is out there looking for my daughter," Mrs. Styles said.

"What am I going to tell the reporters at my door when they ask me how the father takes a vacation while the daughter is with her kidnapper?"

Mrs. Styles pulled Steve's notepad from his pocket, slapped it against the side of the door and scribbled an address. "There!" She threw it in his face.

"I need to know one more thing. Did Emma ever get in trouble with a guy?"

"You mean other than Michael?" Mrs. Styles scorned.

"Someone else."

"No. Emma always kept to herself. She didn't see any one except Michael and his friends. My daughter is not the type to cheat."

"Any idea what this may be?" Steve showed the phone to Mrs. Styles.

Mrs. Styles' eyes widened. "I'm afraid I can't help you, officer." Mrs. Styles said. "Now, let me mourn my daughter in peace."

The door shut on Steve.

***

Jess and Rob showed up at Michael's door.

"About time," Jake said, leading them in.

Jess gave Jake a tight hug.

"Ah … hi," Jake suffocated. Jess let him go with a smile.

"The papers are blowing up with Emma's pictures," Jess said. "I've been running up and down the office building for days. The reporters are saying that Emma was kidnapped. Who would go into the trouble of hiding a car in the woods and meeting with someone on the other end of the highway?"

"Someone she knew," Michael replied. "Does the name Robertson sound familiar to you?"

"You mean like the Robertson pipeline?" Jess took a seat next to Michael.

"I can't seem to find anything about them online," Michael said, looking at his laptop on the coffee table. "It's like the Robertsons don't exist."

"Well, it is a family name, but it doesn't necessarily mean that the family runs it," Jess explained. "Most companies operate like that now."

"Actually, the Robertson pipeline did come up in one assignment," Rob said. "Like a month ago. Something about someone released from jail after working for the Robertson Pipeline for years. They were trying to build it over Native Land, and there were a lot of environmental conflicts. I think that's when the company sold and relocated to Florida."

"Florida…" Michael pondered.

***

"Welcome, brother," a woman greeted Mr. Styles from the front door. "Pardon, my concierge, I sent him home early."

"Where is he?" Mr. Styles walked in. The woman took note of the metal suitcase in his hand.

"Where is who?"

"Don't lie to me, Ava. I know he's here." Mr. Styles heard a whimpering sound above. He headed for the spiral staircase.

"Tommy, you must understand," Ava followed him. "I had to do what I could. To get answers."

He ignored her as he walked into the library. He found a man strapped into a chair with a bleeding face.

He ripped off the tape from the tortured man's face.

"What did you do to him?" Tommy yelled at his sister. "Is this another one of your manipulating games?"

"You got me back into your life when Emma got pregnant," Ava smiled. "As the owner of Robertson Pipeline, I have to step in and take charge of the company heir."

"So, when you said you would take care of the abortion and keep it under wraps, you meant you would keep the baby and raise it to follow in your footsteps?" her brother roared.

"Now, keep it together!" Ava enunciated. "Start acting more like a Robertson."

"That's not who I am," he yelled. "Not anymore. It's been ten years, Ava. Why start this again?"

He looked at the man in the chair. His tears had dried on his cheeks.

"Samantha Cooke was released a month ago," Ava said. "She could be responsible. I had to bring one of her loyal servants." Ava pointed at the man.

"I haven't seen her for ten years," the man sobbed in his chair.

"Oh, get over it." Ava raised her hand and the man closed his eyes. "Pathetic. To think I even had to spend many nights with you to get you to trust me."

"You did what?" her brother yelled.

"You know how it is," Ava scorned. "I seduce the men, and they tell me their darkest secrets."

"You're just like her." He shook his head in disappointment. "I thought I was doing the right thing, selling the company in New York after the disaster the pipeline caused to the Native Land, if only I hadn't fallen for that woman. You were meant for something better, leading this company out of the ditch and starting a new pipeline here, in Florida. What have you been doing all this time? Seducing men and getting them to do your bidding?"

"That's not all I've been doing."

Her brother took out a pocket knife and cut the man's ropes. "You're done here," he said to Ava.

"With him I am," Ava said. "I know where Samantha is."

Chapter 7

The Styles' home was pitch-black. A rattling sound came from an office just down the hall, past the upstairs bathroom. Mrs. Styles pulled on a locked drawer of her husband's desk, furiously trying to break it open. She went into her bedroom and got a black pry bar from under her bed. She had been keeping it safe in case her daughter's kidnapper had broken into the house. It was like New York all over again. She marched back into the office and pried open the drawer. The lock snapped off and the drawer hit the floor. A gun and stacks of paper fell out.

With shaky hands, she grabbed the gun, and loaded it with the bullets from the drawer. Pictures of a young Mrs. Styles with another man in the car fell out from amidst the papers. She flipped one over and it had a phone number on the back. Her hand searched for the phone on the desk; she dialed the number.

***

The old man had finished the rabbit and cleaned up. He tossed a bone with little meat on it to the girl.

"Eat up!" he ordered.

The girl nibbled on it as if hunger had finally hit her.

"I still don't know your name," the girl said.

"Stop asking questions and go to sleep. Don't even think about running in the woods. I know it like the back of my hand. You're more likely to survive by my side than out there." The man laughed.

The girl saw he was missing a tooth.

"Your mom did that," he said. "She was a tough one. What she didn't know, and what you should learn from her, is that when you manipulate men like me, you can end up dead, or worse."

"If you kidnapped me for ransom, how come you haven't called my parents yet? It's been days and we've just been sitting here."

"Because …" the phone rang. The man quickly reached into his jean pocket and pulled it out. "Aha…" he snickered and showed the lit-up flip phone to Emma. "Hi, Lila."

"No …" Emma stirred. Her hands were still taped, and the rope was tied to a tree. She couldn't get anywhere near the man.

"Where is my daughter?" the voice said.

"I missed you, too," the man smirked. "Your daughter's fine. Say hi--"

"Mom!" Emma yelled. "Mom!"

Lila held her breath. She covered her mouth, and let her tears silently fall. "Phil," she said. "I need to see you."

"Well, it's about damn time," he laughed. "Took you long enough. Emma and I were just about to ditch town and hit the city, like old times you and I had."

"Phil, don't—y-you're still in town?"

Phil laughed. "I thought you knew me well enough not to do that."

"Phil, please, my husband he…left, he left me all alone, and I'm scared. I can't do this without you. Please, I need my baby back. I have no one else. You know what that's like. I thought you loved me."

"Still the same… aren't you, Lila."

"Mom! We're in a forest!" Emma yelled. "Just keep going down Highway 6—"

Phil wacked Emma with a log. She passed out against the tree.

"Emma!" Lila yelled on the phone.

"If you want to see your daughter again, come alone, and bring ten mil with you." Phil hung up the phone. He kicked Emma in the gut, rubbed his face and then contained his anger.

***

"This is all I could find in the *Oakland News* database," Jess said from the laptop. She typed quickly and opened up five to six articles that had a mug shot of a woman.

"Samantha Cooke," Michael read. Rob and Jake gathered around. "Arrested for fraud, corruption, terrorism, whoa, this woman is involved with international crime as well."

"You think Emma got involved with someone like her?" Rob asked.

"But, it doesn't make sense." Michael put his face in his hands. "The boot prints we found belong to a man."

"Dude, this woman's got followers everywhere," Jake said, scrolling through his phone. "There's even a blog. Look at all the comments."

Rob took a look at Jake's phone. "Yeah, makes sense. The company illegally profited off of crimes. They rigged scientific evidence that proved their pipeline was harmful to Native Land, destroyed conservation areas, leaking chemicals in the water. This is everything I'm learning in my criminology class."

"The one you and Emma take together?" Michael asked.

"Yeah," Rob nodded. "You think she might have done some digging, found something she shouldn't have?"

"It could be," Jess added. "I would probably go after a lead like that. Stick my nose where it doesn't belong. Geez, if I knew how investigative Emma was I could have set her up with a good gig at *Oakland News*." Jess' eyes widened at an article. "Wait, one of the pipeline construction sites was near Indiana before it shut down a few years ago. A group of workers were convicted of terrorising the neighbors, getting them to move out, so they could expand the pipeline through residential territory."

"How do you know all this?" Jake inquired. "I mean, I know you work with the news and you're pretty smart and all--"

Jess blushed. "My friend's ex-husband was one of those workers. He got arrested many years ago for fraud and terrorism."

"You think he knew Samantha Cooke?" Michael asked.

"Well, they did work for her. The site was being managed under her as the contractor," Jess read in the paper. "But, these are bad people to get involved with."

"That's why we have you," Jake smiled. "You're our best shot at finding Samantha Cooke without getting killed."

"But why would she or her guys go after Emma?" Rob asked.

"Because she's a Robertson," Michael cut in. "She lied to all of us. I'm sorry, guys. I was the one who introduced you to her in high school, and now we're all caught up in her family history. Oh my God!" Michael lurched out of his seat.

"What?" Jake asked.

"Her aunt! Remember her aunt?! What she said? About family history, and money?"

"Dude, you're not making any sense," Jake groaned.

"I'll explain on the way." Michael grabbed his jacket. "Come on, Jess. take us to your friend."

***

"Are you sure this is where Samantha Cooke was last seen?" Tom got out of the car. His sister Ava marched up to the rundown apartment building.

"This doesn't look like a place where she would spend the rest of her life," Tom said.

"She's a convicted criminal, a terrorist," Ava said, searching for the name Cooke on the residents list next to the buzzer. "Where else would she live? Considering her…financial situation."

"That's what we're calling it now?" Tom pushed his sister's hand away as he searched the list. "If she's still smart like she used to be, she would be living under a different name. There." He pointed to a Sophia Alvaro. Ava pushed the buzzer.

"I'm not going to even ask how you knew that," Ava said.

An old lady inside the building stepped out.

"Let me hold that door for you," Tom said.

"You're such a sweetheart," the old lady said, walking out. "Thank you."

Tom and Ava rushed in and headed to the elevator.

"It's good to see you again, brother," Ava said. "It's just like old times." She took out a taser and charged it up to see if it worked.

"Are you seriously going to taser her?" Tom's eyes widened as they got into the elevator."

"Yeah, in case she decides to run."

"She can't outrun us, remember? Someone in prison broke her leg in three places; at least that's what the judge had said during our court meetings."

"That was ten years ago; who knows what she's like now." Ava charged up the taser again and smiled.

They rushed past the apartments and headed to the last one in the corner.

"Wait!" Ava held Tom back. Her eyes pointed to the crack under the door. "We don't want her to see our shadow." Ava took out a pin from her blonde hair. It reminded Tom of his daughter. Ava broke the pin into two and picked the lock.

Tom's jaw dropped.

"There are a number of things that you don't know about your younger sister," Ava said. She unlocked the door and twisted the knob. She put a finger to her lips as she led Tom in behind her.

A rocking chair swayed in front of the TV. Ava checked the rooms. A tea kettle whistled on the stove.

"It's as if she was just here," Ava said.

A scroll bar at the bottom of the screen said, "Emma Styles, a girl of twenty-one, reported missing. Oakland City law enforcement are investigating her kidnapping. If you have any information, contact a police district near you or call---"

"Ava," Tom called. "I think she saw this."

Ava looked at the TV and saw the headline scroll at the bottom. "She knew we were coming. You said her leg was broken, right?"

"The old woman!" Tom exclaimed.

"She couldn't have gone far." Ava ran out the door. Tom followed after her. "Let's take the stairs." They headed down the fire exit and out of the building. They stood in the middle of the road and looked side to side.

"We lost her!" Tom said. "I can't believe I didn't recognize her."

"She must have worn a prosthetic mask. Tom, anyone would have been fooled."

"Not me, Ava; not when I spent many years with her, and now I let her slip past me, again. She's always outsmarted me. I could never beat her at her game. Even when I sold the company, and got her arrested, I still lost, Ava. I lost everything, and now my daughter—"

"You didn't lose everything, Tom," Ava assured. "You still got me."

***

"Thanks for letting us in." Jess led the gang in through the door. A woman in a police uniform welcomed them into her home.

"Officer Becky?" Michael asked.

"That's me." She closed the door after them. "Daniel, say hi to Jess and her friends."

A teenage boy said "hi" from the living room. He was playing a game on his PS3. He aimed at a couple of zombies and shot each one.

"Put it down," Becky said. She ushered her guests to the kitchen dining area. They all sat around the table. "Can I get you some tea?"

"It's okay, I can do it," Jess said. "You go change. I know you only just got home, and it was so kind of you to still let us come."

"Thanks, Jess," Becky side-hugged her friend. "What would I do without you?"

Rob leaned in over Jake. "Is she …?"

"No," Jake whispered back.

Jess knew her way around Becky's kitchen. She set up the mugs and put the kettle on the stove.

"I know Becky from the community center, downtown," Jess explained. "It's a center for troubled women. I go there every week twice or so to hear everyone's story and see if anyone needs help. I try to give self-defense classes sometimes, too. Your girl Emma used to come when she was younger."

"No way; she didn't tell me," Michael said. "But then again, there's a lot she hasn't told us."

Rob put a hand on Michael's back. "I'm sorry, man."

"I didn't know you're such a good member of the community," Jake said to Jess. "Look at you, helping all those women kick ass." Jake playfully punched Jess on the shoulder. She gave him a straight look. "Just kidding." He put his hands up in defense. "Now, I know that with you being Emma's teacher, I'm sure she could kick ass like you. She'll be bringing in her kidnapper all on her own."

"If that was the case, she would have done it already," Michael said, keeping his head in his hands. He moaned. "I'm sorry, Jake. I know you're trying to help, but just stop."

Becky came back down in black tights and a tank top. She had tattoos on the upper part of her arm, and another on her wrist.

"Woah." Jake checked her out. "I'm really digging those…tats."

"Yeah, I wasn't always the good cop," Becky snickered. She grabbed the kettle off the stove and poured tea for everyone. "I really owe it to Jess here, for helping me put my life back together again. I've been trying to get her to join the police force for years."

The boys looked at Jess and tried to imagine her in uniform.

"She could do a lot of good around here."

Jess turned red as everyone smiled at her.

"Underneath all that toughness, she's the most kind-hearted and loving girl I've ever met. Do not be fooled by her appearance," Becky laughed.

Jess played with the pendant around her neck.

"I'm sure anyone would be lucky to have her."

"I am," Jake mumbled, "I mean we all are."

"I don't mean to interrupt the fun we're all having," Michael cut in. "But we need to know where Emma is, and we need your help."

"Michael is right," Jess sighed. "As much as I want this to be a friendly visit, we do have a lot of work to do and it's not just about Emma." Jess peered into the living room to see Daniel still playing his game with his headset on. Jess opened her laptop and showed the articles to Becky, who grabbed a seat next to her.

"I'll show him …" Becky bit her lip. "He would be so capable of doing something like this."

"Do you know his foot size?" Jess asked.

"The print we found in the mud is a size twelve, just a bit over eleven inches," Becky explained. "I have all of Ralph's things packed in boxes in the garage, been wanting to get rid of them, but Daniel wants to keep some of his things, and use them when he's all grown up. I swear if it were up to me--"

"It's okay," Jess assured. "You stay here. You don't have to do that for us, we'll go and take a look, and let you know."

The gang went to the garage and searched through Ralph's things. They found a lot of army knives. Michael hid one in his bag. They found a box of Ralph's boots; they were a size eleven.

"Man, we're so close," Michael said. "We're missing something. Emma wanted the originals from her kidnapper. She was willing to pay a lot for it, and has even risked her life, and been kidnapped for it. Just what is it that she wanted from her kidnapper?"

"Whatever it is, it's not going to be here," Jake said. "We know this Ralph guy wasn't the one who kidnapped her."

"What about this?" Rob held up a checkbook. "If this guy was working for Samantha Cooke, he must have been getting paid. Jess, you think you could get into this guy's account, trace it back to Cooke's? Maybe if we find her we could get our hands on the man she sent after Emma."

"If she's responsible," Jess said. "And yeah, I got someone at *Oakland News* who could do that under the table."

Becky's phone rang on the kitchen table. It was Steve.

"Becky, you finally got through to that phone company," Steve said. "They just emailed you Emma's call history, maybe we can finally take a look at that blocked number and trace it."

"Okay, I'll take a look now." Becky put the phone down. She went on Jess's laptop and logged into her email address. She opened the file and read through the call history, then copied the number from the most recent caller and searched it in the police database.

"It's not a payphone," she mumbled, then searched the phone directories. A profile came up. "Phil Knight," she said. "I'm emailing it to you now, Steve. There's even an address."

From the garage, Jess spoke into her phone. "Stan, can you hack into an account for me?"

"Jess, are you crazy?" Stan answered. "We almost got fired for leaking that news coverage on Emma. We're lucky that

Emma is now officially missing, otherwise *Oakland News* would have had to face charges for false advertising."

"Stan, I wouldn't be asking you if it wasn't urgent," Jess spoke as the boys eavesdropped, continuing their search. "A girl's life is on the line, and you're our only chance of finding her. Please?"

"You owe me," Stan sighed.

"Dinner it is," Jess smiled.

"Who was that?" Jake asked.

"Just a friend." Jess tucked her phone in her pocket.

"Someone's jealous," Rob mumbled.

"What did you say?" Jake asked, and Rob ignored him.

Becky walked into the garage. When she saw her ex-husband's things, she almost gagged. She turned her attention to Jess and handed her back her laptop. "We just got a new lead, so I'm gonna follow up on it with Steve."

"Did you find him?" Michael asked.

"Don't know yet," Becky replied. "I will keep you posted once we check it out. Jess, could you make sure Daniel goes to bed on time? I don't want him to go to school late tomorrow."

"Of course," Jess nodded.

"You're a doll," Becky said, heading back in. She grabbed her uniform and jacket on her way out.

Chapter 8

"Well, the good news is, Emma wasn't with her," Ava said from behind the wheel as she merged in with the cars on the highway.

"The good news?" Tom shouted over the cars honking at them. He grabbed onto the dashboard before his sister could send him flying out the window. "She could be hiding Emma somewhere, for all we know."

"If she was, she wouldn't be heading to the airport right now," Ava said, scrolling through her phone and cutting in line ahead of the honking cars. "She just used her credit card to get a ticket to New York."

Tom took Ava's phone and saw the transaction. "How did you—never mind. There's probably a lot more I don't know about for the last ten years."

"You mean since I put Cooke in jail?" Ava smiled. "Who do you think gathered all the evidence on her? Who hacked into her emails, and bank accounts to save your ass?"

"I don't know what I was thinking." Tom rubbed his head. "I made a mistake. I really thought she loved me. I still don't know how she managed to manipulate me into signing those deals, leaving me with no choice but to sell my company. She covered up those reports pretty well. If I knew our pipeline was damaging the native land and had terrible environmental consequences; I would've put an end to it. I'm just glad you're running it now. You're doing a much better job than I ever did."

"Is this your way of saying sorry?" Ava snickered. "I've forgiven you already. A long time ago. It's about time you've forgiven yourself."

"You're right." Tom grabbed his sister's hand. "I should've called you more often. I'm sorry."

"After all this is done, and we find Emma, you're all spending the summer at my house."

"Deal."

***

Jess received a text message on her phone and gathered the boys together. "It's here," she said, clicking on a link. "Looks like Cooke's on her way to New York."

Jake, Rob, and Michael saw the booking information on Jess' phone.

"Well, what are we doing? Let's go." Michael zipped up his jacket and opened the garage door. Everyone's eyes landed on Rob's car.

"You mean we're driving?" Jake's jaw dropped.

"In my car?" Rob asked.

Michael took Rob's keys and got into the car. "She's our only lead to finding Emma. Now, come on."

Rob rolled his eyes and grabbed a box of cereal off a shelf against the garage wall, and a jug of milk from a refrigerator. "Might as well have breakfast on the way there."

Jess sat in the passenger seat and chartered a course to Cooke's address. "She still has her old apartment. She's probably gonna head there once her plane lands in two hours."

***

Steve and Becky sat in his office looking at Phil Knight's file.

"He looks so familiar," Steve said, bringing Phil Knight's photo close to his face. "Why would he be after the Styles' kid? What does he have on them?"

"He was my high school boyfriend," a voice said.

Steve and Becky looked up to see Lila walk into the office. "He's got her, Steve. I need your help."

"Phil!" Steve slammed his hand down on Phil's picture. "That Phil? You dated the guy who always got in trouble for stealing people's cars? You know I caught him dealing drugs with a local gang once."

"I know," Lila admitted, averting her eyes. Her hands shook as she held her purse tight to her chest. "He's dangerous.

"I got a location," Becky said, looking from the computer. "Just off of Highway 6—"

"64," Lila answered. "It's where we used to hang out."

"Why would he make it so easy to find him?" Becky wondered. "This could be a trap."

"He knows I'm coming," Lila explained. "He wants me to find him. He wants me, Steve. I need to go in alone."

"Lila." Steve folded his hands over his desk. "Why did you come to the cops, if he told you not to?"

"Because I trust you."

***

The man with the scar on his face snapped his phone in two. "Won't be needing this anymore," he said, kicking it into the earth. "Your mother better show up without the cops, or you're dead." He seized Emma's mouth and pushed her head against a tree.

Emma slid down the side of the tree and hugged her legs. She shivered from the cold as she watched the man sit by the fire. He rummaged through a bag of CDs, portable hard drives, and stacks of pictures. He started to laugh.

"Did you really think you'd burnt the last of them?" he asked. "Didn't you think I'd have more online copies?" He held bundles of bills tied together by an elastic band and sniffed it. "This is never gonna be enough. You and your mother won't be able to get rid of me that easy. I can always come back for more whenever I want. You should be careful next time not to manipulate men like me. I'd think you would've learned from your mom by now, but I guess she didn't learn her lesson yet either. You look just like her when she was your age."

Emma's eyes widened. "You knew my mother at the university?"

"We were high school sweethearts," the man spat.

"My mother would've never dated a man like you!"

"Oh, she did. More than just dating," the man smirked. "She lived on the streets like I did. Pickpocketing, stealing from the rich, eating from the trash, your mother and I loved the street life. She sought danger far more than I ever did. She was the mastermind, I was the muscle."

"That's not true!" Emma shouted. "My mother grew up in Oakland. She had the best grades in school. I've seen the pictures, and you weren't in any of them."

"Don't you see?" The man stared into Emma's eyes. "Your mother has lied to you, too. Your father, Tom Robertson, was just another job, another man to seduce and rob, until she took it too far, got pregnant with you, and had no choice but to marry the guy. It was the only way she could afford to raise you. Your whole life was a lie. It's only a shame that I wasn't part of it."

"You're lying!" Emma lunged at the man and knocked him down on his back. He grabbed her by the collar and was ready for a fight but froze when he saw tears roll down her cheeks. He looked at her as though he'd seen them before.

Chapter 9

Ava and Tom ran into the airport, searching for Cooke in her disguise as the old woman from the apartment. They were in the terminal as crowds of people shoved through them. Announcements were on replay, warning passengers of the last call for a number of flights. One was for New York. Ava darted toward the check-in desk, as attendants were getting ready to leave.

"I need to get on this flight!" she demanded while Tom followed her.

"Ma'am, the gate is closing," the attendant said. "No one can enter anymore. Besides, the flight is booked. You'll have to get on the next one."

"Do you know who you're talking to?!" Ava raised her voice and a few bystanders eyed her.

"Lower your voice," Tom whispered into Ava's ear. "This would look bad for the company." Tom looked at the attendant and asked, "When is the next plane?"

***

Michael drove down the highway, his arms stiff, his face pale, and his eyes dreary. Jess looked behind to see Rob and Jake sleeping with their heads resting on each other's.

"Let me drive," Jess said. "You've been at it for five hours nonstop."

"I can't," Michael said. "I have to keep going. I can't go to sleep now."

"If you keep going at this rate, you're going to get us all killed. How are we gonna get there, if you can't even drive properly?"

"It was just a bird," Michael moaned. "I didn't want to hit it. Besides, that was ages ago, I can still drive."

"Michael, there was no bird," Jess enunciated. "You must have dozed off and dreamt about that. Now, pull over to the side and let me drive."

A light flickered on the dashboard. Michael was low on fuel. He smiled and pulled into the next exit heading toward the gas station. As soon as the car came to a stop, Jess got out of the car and helped Michael out. He hadn't realized that he'd been sitting for five hours without moving. His whole body ached, and as Jess woke up Rob and Jake for a bathroom break, Michael passed out in the back seat.

"You want me to get that?" Jake asked Jess as she fuelled up the car.

"You're paying?" Jess raised her eyebrows at him.

"Well, yeah," Jake smiled. "And I want to meet this Stan guy. Tell him Jake is stopping by after all this is over."

"Okay," Jess laughed.

"Dude." Rob nudged Jake as they headed into the station. "I've never seen Jess laugh like that with anyone except for you. With a big gal like that, I doubt anyone could make her even budge."

"She's not that scary," Jake said, but after Rob eyed him for a few seconds, he admitted, "Okay, she can be intimidating sometimes, but she's really all soft on the inside once you get to know her." Jake headed down an aisle and picked up a granola bar. "So, what's the deal between you and Vanessa?"

"Nothing," Rob stated, annoyed. He grabbed a Coke from the fridge and opened it.

"It's clearly not nothing. You two live together, there's no way that nothing happened between you two."

"Why does everyone say that?"

"Cause she's hot, and smart, wants to be a doctor, like you. She's totally in your league."

"She's a liar and a manipulative bitch. I know not to get involved with people like that."

"The fact that you know that means something really did happen between you too. Come on, tell me. Don't spare the details."

Rob looked back to see Jess still pumping gas into the car. He bent down to Jake's ear and said, "Let's just say, been there done that—"

"You didn't?" Jake's eyes beamed.

"It was unpleasant, and a big mistake that will never, I mean ever, happen again." Rob took a sip from his coke. "I would be totally cool with it if you wanted to see her, but I wouldn't recommend it."

"No, man. I knew there was something between you two from the start. You fight like a married couple."

Juice snorted out of Rob's nose.

"You think I didn't know what she was trying to do, kissing me like that in front of you guys?"

Rob wiped his face with his hand and groaned at the sight of his drenched shirt. "What?"

"She was trying to make you jealous, man. You should totally date her. You two could have so much fun in med school and be doctors together. You could practically live together in a hospital."

"I would kill myself if I did."

"Come on." Jake rubbed Rob's shoulders. "Lighten up. How hard could it be?"

"You guys gonna pay for that?" A woman stuck her head over the counter. She stood behind the cashier waiting for Jake and Rob to pay for their snacks. "You gonna cover that too?" She pointed at the car.

"Yeah." Jake reached into his pocket.

"That will be twenty dollars."

Jake put a twenty on the counter.

"Plus two for that granola bar."

"What? It's only a buck back at where I work."

"Well, this is my gas station, and that bar is two dollars here."

Jake rolled his eyes and cocked his head at Rob. Rob reached into his pocket and dropped two dollar bills. Jake and Rob headed into the car as Jess sat in the driver's seat. Rob nudged Jake to get into the front while he sat in the back with Michael.

"How many hours left?" Jake asked Jess, handing her a granola bar.

"Oh wow, you remembered." Jess took it.

"Well, you know what they say, keep the driver happy, and we'll get there faster."

"Who says that?" Jess laughed.

"I do. I just made it up."

Rob watched them from the back and smiled. After they left Ohio, and were approaching Pennsylvania, it started to rain.

"Any updates on where Cooke is now?" Rob asked. "She probably landed hours ago."

"Check my phone," Jess told Jake.

"Where is it?" Jake asked.

"In my pocket," Jess explained.

"Okay." Jake eyed Jess up and down and hesitated.

"Just take it out!"

"Okay!" Jake reached for Jess' pocket.

"Not this one," she said. "The other one."

Jake closed his eyes as his arm hovered over Jess' legs to the other side of her thigh. He felt for her pocket, pulled the phone out, opened his eyes and exhaled. His face was so close to Jess' and the sound of a honking car jerked Jake away. Jess pulled out of the other lane before crashing into other oncoming cars.

"That was close," she sighed.

"Too close," Jake mumbled, panting as he rested his back into his seat. He turned the phone on, putting in Jess' password—her birthday. "Got it," he said. "She took an Uber to Queens. I got the address here."

"Perfect." Jess said. "Only four more hours to go. Let's hope she'll still be there when we arrive."

***

Ava and Tom sat on a plane in silence. Ava kept checking her watch and looking out the window.

"What's taking them so long?" she asked, pressing a button on her screen. The lights above lit up signalling for the attendant's help. "This darn service here in economy. I told you we should've taken first class. Nobody seems to notice us here."

"Those were the only seats available," Tom said. "It's only a two-hour flight. Do you get first class all the time?"

"Of course." Ava crossed her arms and settled into her seat. "You used to do it too."

"It's been ten years since I stopped living that kind of life."

"Then what kind of life have you been living?"

107

"You know, it didn't take me that long to adjust to this," Tom said, grabbing the handle of his seat. "It's just easier, knowing that you have nothing left to lose. How do you do it, Ava? Don't you worry every night about the company, where it's going, whether a report on the pipeline's environmental effects will land on your desk tomorrow? How do you keep it all together? These past ten years have given me the best sleep in my life."

"Me keeping the company altogether has given you the best sleep of your life?" Ava watched the workers outside, waving for the plane to back up. "I, on the other hand, like to take out my stress differently." She tapped her fist against her palm. "Someone better explain what's taking so long or I'm getting on a private jet."

"Didn't we used to have one of those?" Tom commented.

"Yeah, until I ransacked it last week, going after Cooke's dogs. Can't believe they're still loyal to her after ten years. I'm sure she's got someone in New York now with Emma. She's going to lead us right to her."

"You think it might be a trap?" Tom asked. "It seemed like she knew we were coming last time. She probably knows we're onto her by now."

"Even if she did, it'll be too late for her to hide. I already called some of my men from New York to head over to Queens." Ava showed Tom her phone. "Their gonna keep an eye on her until we get there. I want to be the one to take her down this time."

***

Lila sat in the backseat of Steve's police car, as he and Becky were in the front. Rain pelted onto the windshield and the car swerved on the highway.

"Let me make it clear to you again, Steve," Lila explained. "I go in alone. You and Officer Becky stay here. I have you on speed dial. I will ring for you to make the arrest only once Emma is safe."

Steve gave Becky a look, while Becky looked at Lila from the sideview mirror.

"I'm not making any promises," Steve said. "If he's been after you for so long, he's going to be well prepared. And if he knows you really well, like you say he does, he probably knows we're going to be here too."

"You're wrong, Steve," Lila said. "I never got cops involved before. I know Phil better than anyone. He still loves me, and I will use that against him, as I've always done. He always wanted more and using him to make Tom jealous at the time, was not enough for him. When Tom stopped noticing me, and kept seeing that damn woman all the time, he didn't even care about where I was and who I was with. So, I gave up; cancelled everything with Phil. I even paid him off to stay away." She kicked a bag at her feet. "He'll think I brought more money for him, but don't worry. He's not going to get his hands on it. I have a plan."

"So, you say." Steve gripped the wheel, peeking through the windshield to see past the rain. "So, you've just been paying him off all this time. Didn't you think about coming to the cops when the money ran out?"

"When my money ran out, of course, I never used Tom's, and I couldn't manipulate Phil anymore either, so he tried to hurt me. I had no choice but to tell Tom the truth. Our world was falling apart, and our daughters'. He threatened to come after her next if I didn't pay up. Tom wasn't convinced, either. He was so caught up into that damn woman's lies, he had to sell his company, and we had to change our names, move out of New York, and start a new life here in Oakland."

"Cutting off ties with Phil, completely," Officer Becky added. "You know my ex-husband worked for your company."

"Easy," Steve advised.

Officer Becky turned to look Lila in the eye. "He got paid under the table to do your husband's dirty work."

"It wasn't him," Lila shook her head. "It was that damn woman."

"Cooke, right?" Officer Becky added. "You say she's responsible for everything, but it was your husband who signed the papers. He must've been in on it too. He shouldn't hide behind a woman. He should be a man and face the law."

Lila slapped Officer Becky. "Don't you dare talk about my husband like that."

"Congratulations. You've just assaulted an officer, all the more reason to arrest you, and take down your husband next."

"Becky!" Steve shouted. "What's gotten into you today? I need you on top of all this. We got a man to take down. We've all got to stay sharp. Can't be losing it now."

"My husband was manipulated by that woman, just as your husband let himself be manipulated by the money," Lila added after a few moments of silence. "We both lost a lot that day. Believe me, I understand. I may not have a son, but I do have a daughter, and girls are always harder to understand."

***

"Is this the place?" Jake looked at a townhouse from the window of the car.

Jess took the key out of the ignition and checked her phone. "This is the right house."

"So, what do we do now? It's not like we can just walk in," Michael said. "If Emma's in there, we need a plan."

"I agree." Rob nodded. "Who's to say she isn't waiting for us in there. She could be armed and using Emma as hostage."

"We could go in through that window." Jess pointed to the second floor. There was an open window where they could easily crawl over the shingles of the roof and into the house. "I can push someone up. Any volunteers?" Jess looked at the backseat and followed Michael and Rob's gaze to Jake.

"Why does it always have to be me?" he groaned. Getting out of the car, he pulled over his hoodie and rubbed his hands together.

They headed over to the garage door, and Michael pushed Jake onto Jess and Rob's shoulders. He climbed onto the roof and stretched his arms down to help the rest up. They crawled through the window and landed onto the dusty carpet.

"It's so quiet in here," Jake whispered.

Michael popped his head into one of dark rooms. "Emma?" He found a bed and a dresser covered in sheets layered with dust.

"These rooms are also empty," Rob said, coming out of another room that had covered furniture.

"Let's check downstairs." Jess guided the rest of the crew down the staircase. As soon as they reached the living room, the lights flickered on. They all turned to find an old woman sitting in a rocking chair with her hand resting on a bedside table with a lamp.

"Can I help you?" she asked.

"Samantha Cooke?" Jess asked.

The woman untied her hair, and pulled on the skin over her face, revealing a younger and smoother skin underneath. "It was part of my disguise, I was expecting someone else, you see."

"Where's Emma?" Michael demanded. "Where are you keeping her?"

"Emma? Mmm, I don't recall."

"The Robertsons! You worked with them."

"Now, that I remember."

"There's no one here." Rob shook his head, coming out of the kitchen. Jake followed in after him.

"The garage is clear too," he added.

"Where are you keeping her?!"

"Michael, calm down." Jess rested her palm on his shoulder.

"You must be the boyfriend." Cooke laughed. "What makes you think I have her?"

"To get your revenge, for what the Robertsons did to you."

"More like for Tom leaving me." Cooke stood up from her chair and whacked Michael with a cane. Jess helped him up.

"You see, your girlfriend has manipulated you just as Tom did to me," Cooke continued.

"That's not what the papers say," Jess cut in. "You got Tom to do your bidding, you orchestrated all these construction sites, bribed the workers to build the pipeline on unstable grounds, the chemical leaks; all of it was you."

"Really? And who do you supposed paid and signed for all of it?"

The boys exchanged a look between Jess and Cooke. Jess' fists tightened at her side while Cooke had her cane ready.

"The Robertsons are just as guilty as I am." Cooke dropped her cane and reached for a bottle of vodka on the table. She pulled out a drawer of medication and emptied a bottle into her hand. "Who's going to believe a psychotic woman anyway, especially one who just got released from an asylum?" She popped the pills into her mouth and drank from the bottle as she sat back down in her rocking chair. "Emma's not here, and I doubt you're ever going to find her." She laughed hysterically. "Take it from me, the Robertsons already changed their name once, who's to say they won't do it again? What? You think just because Tom and I had an affair, I would kidnap his daughter to get him to be with me again? That would be a good plan, except I never loved Tom, it was purely just business. Whatever he told you was a lie."

"I can't believe this." Michael ran his hand through his hair. "You're lying! You took Emma, and this is all just a game to you!"

Jess held Michael back before he could attack Cooke.

"You have no proof." Cooke laughed. "If Emma's not here, then you have no reason to stay."

"Let's just go," Jake whispered into Michael's ear.

"What?!" Michael pushed Jess' hand away from his head. It was covered in blood.

"This woman's a psycho," he added. "Who knows what she's going to do next. I don't want to get beat up by her."

Jess gave him a look.

"What? Is it so wrong to want to avoid picking a fight with a woman?" Jake pulled Michael up on his feet. "Let's get out of here. This was all a waste of time."

"I'm afraid he's right," a voice spoke from the front door. As the figure walked into the light of the living room, her face lit up and a smile spread across her face. "I can take it from here."

"Mr. Styles?" the boys said at the same time.

"Michael, are you all right?" Tom noticed the blood from Michael's head. "What did you do to him?!" he yelled at Cooke, surprised to see how much she had changed. Cooke took another sip from her bottle and laughed nonstop.

"She's out of her mind!" Jake yelled. "Emma's not here. Come on," Jake urged the rest to leave with him.

"Hold on." Tom stood in his way. "What do you mean Emma's not here?"

Ava rolled up her sleeves and pulled on Cooke's hair. "Speak up!"

Cooke knelt down and picked up her cane, still caught up in her maniac state, and swung it at Ava's feet. Ava lost her balance and pulled Cooke down with her. The two sprawled onto the floor, banging fists into each other's faces.

"Enough!" Tom shouted, pulling the two apart. "I want the truth, Cooke; where's my daughter?"

Cooke spat blood onto the floor and wiped her lips. "You're not the only one with secrets. Your wife is too."

Ava straightened her back and fixed her collar.

"Geez, is it always like this with you women?" Jake mumbled. He placed Michael's arm over his shoulder and they walked out the door.

"I'm putting everyone back on a flight to Indiana," Tom announced. "And you," he grasped Cooke's arm, "belong back in that there asylum, where we left you."

Cooke freed her arm, grabbed for the bottle again, and sipped it from her chair. "I'll be waiting for you in hell."

Tom helped Ava up, and Rob and Jess followed them to the door. They found Michael and Jake waiting by the car.

"We still got my old jet?" Tom asked his sister, getting her into the cab that waited near Rob's car.

"I'll make a call and find out," Ava said.

"All of you are coming as well." Tom looked to the others. "Now, get in and let's go find Emma."

Chapter 10

“Turn here,” Lila instructed Steve. Steve veered the car into the exit, and they went into a forested path through caved-in trees. The rain hammered against the windows and lightening lit the sky a number of times. “It should be here,” she said, eying the clouds. There was just a bit under an hour before the sun would set. “You need to hurry before it gets dark, or there’s no way you’re coming out of that forest.”

“All right, all right,” Steve said.

“Don’t stop until you pass a sign that says White Rock,” Lila said. “They should be just past that.”

***

“Do you still love my mom?” Emma asked, watching the man set up a tent over their heads as it rained.

“It’s been ten years since I last saw her,” the man explained, hammering the tent pole into the soil. Emma had her hands tied to the other pole, and she twisted her thumb back to her wrist at a failed attempt to free her from it.

The man stared at her in doubt. "What did you just do?" He checked the ropes, making sure they were still tight.

"I'm double jointed," Emma said. "Relax."

The man took Emma's thumb and bent it back. "This doesn't hurt?"

"Let me go." Emma fought back. "Please! If you still love my mom, do it for her."

"I can't believe this." The man shook his head in disbelief.

"Can't believe what?"

The man kicked the bag of tapes to the ground. In frenzy, he lifted a log and threw it against a tree. Emma screamed as she watched the man lose his mind.

"Your mother has ruined my life!" he shouted.

"No, Phil," a voice answered. "You have!"

"Mom?" Emma called from inside the tent. "Is that you?"

The man turned his head toward Lila's direction, who was pointing a gun at him.

"Put it down," Lila demanded as the man dropped a tent pole from his hand.

"Easy, Lila," Phil said, putting his hands up.

"Where's Emma?"

"She's right here, right here." Phil turned to the tent and heard a click.

"Slowly," Lila said.

Phil untied Emma and dragged her out of the tent by her hair.

"Mom!" Emma cried and froze when her eyes landed on the gun.

"You've been keeping her from me this whole time, Lila," Phil said. "I know the truth. You see this?" Phil bent Emma's thumb back as she sobbed. "She got that from me. You thought I wouldn't know? You lied to me, Lila! She lied to you!" he shouted into Emma's ear.

"She's not your daughter, Phil." Lila's face stiffened, and her eyes fixed on her daughter's tears. "You could never be a father to her."

"We could have had a life together! I would've changed if you had told me."

"You loved the streets too much, Phil; we both know that's not true. It's too late. Now, give me back my daughter, let her go or I'm going to shoot you."

Phil let go of Emma's hair and pushed her toward her mom. Emma ran to her mother and hugged her while Lila kept her gun pointed at Phil.

"You okay, sweetie?" she whispered. "Did he hurt you?"

"I'm fine," Emma sobbed.

Lila noticed one of Emma's cheeks was red and swollen. She then sees a tape on the soil with a bundle of money next to it. "Tell me why I shouldn't just end you right here and now?" Lila threatened Phil. "All it would take is one pull of this trigger, and then we don't have to see you ever again."

"No, please, mom." Emma pulled on her mother's arm. "Let him go."

"You think I came all the way here for this?" He stomped onto the tapes, crushing them under his heel. "I just wanted to talk."

"By kidnapping my daughter?"

"I made a mistake," Phil explained. "I thought if I exposed our affair to the public, Tom wouldn't be able to live with you in shame. He'd dump you and you'd come back running to me. You know you are so much better than him."

"You're wrong, Phil. Tom would never leave me, even if you leaked all that to the news."

"Really?" Phil laughed hesitantly. "Because that's not what you told me ten years ago, when he found out the truth."

"I'm so sorry, mom," Emma apologized. "I just wanted to pay him off and destroy all the tapes, so you and Dad wouldn't get a divorce. You almost did before, and I couldn't live with that."

"It's okay, sweetie." Lila kissed Emma's head. "It'll all be over soon." Turning her eyes back to Phil, she said, "goodbye, Phil." She pulled the trigger and Emma pushed her mom down to the ground.

"Run!" Emma yelled at Phil.

Phil covered his ears from the sound of the gun, glad for the bullet to have missed him, and ran into the woods. Lila screamed as her hands scurried for the gun. Emma kicked it away and hugged her mom.

"What happened?" Steve, with a rifle in hand, came running down the hill with Becky. They reached Emma and her mother. "You had a gun?" Steve yelled. "What were you thinking?" His eyes scanned for Phil in the forest and Becky went to search for him.

"He's gone," Emma said.

Steve lowered his rifle and stretched his arms open as Emma hugged him. She buried her head into his chest and sobbed.

"Come on, let's get you home," he said.

Becky came back after a few moments, shaking her head. It was getting dark, and she helped Steve take Emma and her mom back to the car. As they drove in the rain, Lila hugged her daughter, her tears flowing onto Emma's hair. Emma remained still, her eyes solemn with tears. She didn't move or speak. After an hour of silence, the car pulled into the Styles' driveway just as Tom, Ava, and Emma's friends ran out of the front door to greet them. Tom darted for the door and pulled Emma close to him as he cried. Ava followed in after him, and Tom introduced her to Emma. They hugged each other in a circle, as Michael and his friends stood watching.

"We found her," Jake said to Michael. "She's really still alive."

"And you're really going to be a dad," Rob teased. "You must be so relieved."

Michael remained still, his gaze unmoving.

"Michael, are you okay?" Jess asked.

Steve pulled a receiver from his car and brought it close to his mouth. "I'm going to need everyone alert for Phil Knight, I repeat, Phil Knight for kidnapping. He was last seen running through White Rock forest, just off the exit of Highway 64."

Michael and his friends listened in on the news, and Jess met up with Becky to catch up on what happened. When Tom and Lila released Emma from their embrace, Emma's eyes caught Michael's. He approached her.

"Now is not a good time," Lila cut in.

"Are you okay?" Michael asked, ignoring Lila. "Why did you lie to me, Emma? I could've helped you! I could've been there for you!" Michael rested a hand on Emma's stomach. "Is it true? Is our baby really in there?"

Tears rolled down Emma's cheeks. "I'm sorry, Michael."

"Come on, sweetheart, let's go inside." Lila wrapped her arms around Emma and they walked to the door.

"It's best you keep your distance," Tom warned Michael. "She's already been through enough."

"Hey, we went a long way looking for her, he deserves to see her," Jake complained.

"Yeah, and after all the classes I've missed, I doubt I'm getting into med school," Rob added. "We can't let that go to waste."

"It's okay," Michael interrupted. "I understand. I'll go."

"They're not going to press charges?" Jess' voice echoed from behind as she talked to Becky.

"It's best if we just leave it alone," Becky insisted, trying to get Jess to lower her voice.

"Thank you, Steve." Tom shook Steve's hand from the car and headed inside.

"Come on, Michael," Jake tapped him on the shoulder. "I'll drive you."

Rob gave him a look.

"Oh, right. Your car's still in New York. Guess we're going to have to make another trip there. What do you say, Michael? Bring Emma a long too. once she's all better."

"That's a great, idea," Rob added. "You two have been planning to go there anyway, for the summer."

"Yeah, it's a plan," Jake said.

***

A newspaper landed on a desk, five months after the incident. It read, *The Robertsons Reunite for a Summer in Florida.*

"That's just great." Jess looked up from her desk at Stan. "Am I really going to have to fly out there and get a comment from them? I thought I was on sports this week."

"Oh, come on, you and Jake could take a trip there," Stan said.

"Me and Jake?" Jess' jaw dropped.

"Oh, come on, everybody sees it. You two have had a lot going on since you were kids."

Jess' cheeks turned red. "It's really that obvious?"

"Look, he walks in here every other day with a cup of coffee and those granolas you like to snack on, and every time I walk in here to tell you he's out there, you just start giggling like a little girl. No offense."

"None taken," Jess snickered, dumping the paper into her bag. "I'll get on it." She headed out her office and turned to give Stan one more look. "Thanks, Stan…for understanding."

Back at Michael's home, his mother placed a plate of scrambled eggs on the table in front of Michael.

"You should eat something," she urged. "It's been five months."

"Five months and nothing," Michael said. "She won't see me. She won't answer her calls. We're supposed to be having a baby together, for God's sake. At least I thought we were, and now she's off in Florida, having the time of her life." Michael dropped today's paper next to his plate.

"I know dear," his mother comforted. "I'm sure she's just traumatized from it all. She'll come when she's ready."

"If she was really traumatized, how come it says here that she forgives the guy who did this?" Michael read from the paper. "He's had a tough life as it is, and that's punishment enough? Who says that? What about me? Hasn't she punished me enough? She's probably happy to go back to her old life, all rich and famous again. She doesn't want anything to do with me anymore."

"That's not true."

A knock came on the door.

"Oh, I'll get it." Michael's mother wiped her hands on her apron. "It's probably the reporters again, wanting to know what it was like dating a Robertson, and getting her knocked up. I told them so many times that you had no idea who she was, and you didn't get her knocked up so you could get a share of her money." Michael's mother headed out the kitchen and opened the door. "My God!" she gasped. Michael pushed his chair back and walked over to see what happened. His eyes widened as he stared out the door.

"Emma?" Michael gulped. "What are you doing here?"

A smile formed on Michael's mother and she mouthed, "I told you," as she gave them some privacy.

Michael noticed the protruding belly from Emma. Her hair drooped down to her waist. "You look different," he said. "Aren't you supposed to be in Florida?"

"I was, but I couldn't go. I had to come see you."

"Me?" Michael rested his palm against the door frame. "After five months? It's okay, I get it. Now that you're rich and famous again, why would someone like you want anything to do with me?"

"Michael," Emma panted.

"First, I get you pregnant and it's all my fault, I get it. But, then you take off and tell me you'll be back soon, only to find out you were kidnapped by some guy, who turns out to be your biological father—"

"Michael," Emma urged. Her arms wrapped around his shoulders and she buried her head into his neck.

"Oh, so now, you want to get back with me."

"The baby," she whispered into his ear. "It's coming." Her eyes rolled to the back of her head and she fainted.

"Mom!" Michael shouted.

"I know, I heard, I heard!" She came running toward them with a phone in hand. "I called nine-one-one. The reporters are going to flip over this."

"There's no time, let's get her into the car." Michael's mother helped him carry Emma into his car.

"I'll drive." Michael's mother took the keys from him. "You just stay with her and help her concentrate on her breathing."

Emma groaned in the back seat as Michael sat down next to her.

"Come on, Emma," he tapped her on her cheek. "You can do this." He squeezed her hand. The smell of her hair reminded him of their last time together, the morning after she woke up in his bed, the morning before they got into another one of their fights. "Oh my God, we're really having a baby. It's really happening. I'm going to be a dad! I'm going to be a dad!"

Emma screamed as the car pulled into the hospital. The nurses wheeled her in to the ER and they quickly put on some scrubs and throwing a gown at Michael. Michael fiddled for his phone, texting the group, just before another nurse snatched it away. "Let's go Mr. Danes," she said. "We don't have all day."

As Emma lay in the delivery room, screaming at the top of her lungs, sweat dripped from Michael's hair as he squeezed his eyes shut and screamed along with Emma. "Oh my God, just breathe, just breathe."

Jake and Jess, along with Rob and Vanessa, arrived at the waiting room. They saw Michael's mother talking on the phone.

"She wasn't due for another few weeks," Lila's voice screamed from the phone.

"Well, you better come now, or you're going to miss the birth of your grandchild," Michael's mother said. "Oh, Jake, thank God you're here." She tossed him the phone and hugged Jess. "Oh, you look so beautiful, dear, as always. And who's this young woman?" She eyed Vanessa.

"Oh, she's my girlfriend." Rob smiled.

"Good for you!" Michael's mother hugged him and Vanessa.

"So, according to the MCAT, there are a number of medical consequences to delivering a baby weeks in advance," Vanessa said, scrolling through her phone. "I would be happy to go over them with you one by one, so you can be prepared."

"I don't think she needs this right now," Rob whispered into Vanessa's ear. "I'm sorry, she's always like this," he said to the others.

"It's a girl!" Michael barged in through the doors and announced to everyone in the waiting room.

"Oh my God!" Michael's mother ran to hug him.

"You can see her now," a doctor informed them. They all hurried to the nursery.

"That's her over there." Michael pointed to the third baby in the second row of other babies.

"Do you have a name for the little angel?" a nurse asked, holding a clipboard.

"Oh, we didn't—at least not yet. I'll go ask Emma." Michael kissed his mother on the cheek and went to check on Emma.

"He's never done that," Michael's mother told everyone with a big smile on her face. "She looks like a Michelle," she said, looking at the baby from the glass window. "When I was having Michael, I was going to call him Michelle, until I found out he was a boy."

Michael knocked on Emma's door and walked in. She was resting in bed, her face pale, and her arm hooked up to an IV.

"She looks just like you," he said, taking a seat next to her. He grasped her hand and kissed it. Emma pulled her hand away and Michael pulled tighter. "I'm not going to let you go. Not this time. I'll do everything to provide for this family and raise our child together. Please marry me, Emma. If you can't do that for me, do it for her?"

Tears rolled down Emma's cheeks as she smiled. "I'm so sorry, Michael. I kept you out of this for so long."

"It's okay." Michael kissed Emma's forehead. "It's all over now."

"I'm just scared. I don't want our child to grow up to be like me or the manipulative women in my family. I don't want her to be a Robertson."

"She'll be a Danes," Michael assured, wiping Emma's tears as she chuckled. "She'll be even better than a Danes or a Robertson. You'll see."

"There she is." Jess barged in through the door, as the room filled with Michael's friends and his mother. "I've already got your daughter signed up for defense classes. She's going to be one tough lady, you'll see."

Everyone laughed.

"So, you didn't answer my question," Michael said to Emma.

"What question?" Jake asked.

Emma sat up, and clasped Michael's hand in hers. "I do."

The End